LIZZY GAYLE

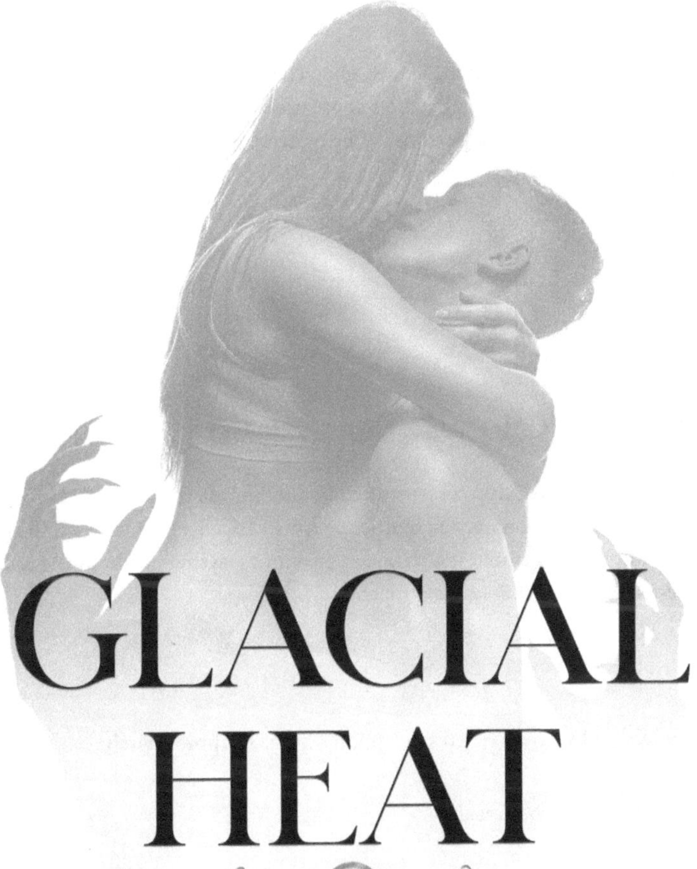

GLACIAL HEAT

A FANTASY RESORTS NOVEL

MYSTIC OWL

AN IMPRINT OF CITY OWL PRESS

GLACIAL HEAT
Fantasy Resorts, Book 3

MYSTIC OWL
A City Owl Press Imprint
www.cityowlpress.com

Cover Design by MiblArt. All stock photos licensed appropriately.

Edited by Heather McCorkle.

For information on subsidiary rights, please contact the publisher at info@cityowlpress.com.

Print Edition ISBN: 978-1-64898-348-1

Digital Edition ISBN: 978-1-64898-349-8

Printed in the United States of America

To Heather for all your encouragement and guidance. And because you love the cold!

1

ROSI

My poor little heart raced faster than the supersonic jet whipping us across the world. Glancing at Cora only made my anxiety worse. My best friend was on her third tiny bottle of rum and second can of cola, a canary-yellow bikini strap visible beneath the ruffled sleeve that slipped down her shoulder. She swayed to the music in her head without an ounce of self-consciousness, whipping her multicolored hair back and forth in time to something only she could hear.

When she opened her eyes to take another swig, she noticed me staring and shook her head.

"I thought you'd relax once we left LA, but here's Rosi, looking pale as a vampire, and as rigid as one who's been staked up the ass."

"Thanks," I groaned, checking to see if anyone else in first class heard her. It would've been a miracle if no one had since Cora had the loudest voice ever.

"It's a very long stake. Like a big ole flagpole." She snorted before guzzling the remainder of her plastic cup.

I chewed on a stray curl, completely aware I was restarting a habit I'd kicked long ago.

Cora batted it out of my mouth and leaned in, wafting rum flavored breath all over me.

"This is the vacation of a lifetime. Would you please at least try and relax?" She pulled me to her side and ground her knuckles on my scalp a bit too hard. "You won this trip for a reason. It was meant to be. It was literally in the cards—remember that Tarot spread I did right before you got the call?"

Leaning on her shoulder, I blocked her hand from messing further with my head. "You said, 'Good news,' as I recall. Not exactly, 'You win a trip to a fantasy resort in Greenland.'"

"The cards said both our lives were transforming. We are coming out of our chrysalises on this trip."

I shuddered at the memory of Cora overturning the Death card the morning I'd gotten the call about winning the trip. Her interpretation was great, but no denying the giant, gilded word splayed across the front shook me.

It was a good thing Cora was the psychic. Even though I believed in the strange, I'd never shown any personal gifts before, and after the night I had not forty-eight hours prior, I didn't want to consider having developed a sudden talent featuring prophetic nightmares.

The dream that hadn't felt like a dream flashed through my mind in crystal clarity: the snarl, the blur of mottled skin, then the stench of something rotting, but most of all the stark contrast of dark red running in rivulets across the pristine snow.

Blinking, I tightened my grip on my armrest and shoved the images out of my mind, only to realize seconds later we'd been swaying to Cora's music again while her eyes were closed. I pulled away.

"Thanks, *chica*. I feel better now. I'm glad they let me bring a plus-one."

Cora grinned. "Me too! Have I thanked you yet? Because this is cray-cray. I've never won anything in my life." She motioned for another bottle of rum and a can of cola.

I grabbed her hand and lowered it to the armrest between us. "Whoa there. If I don't cut you off, you won't remember the Glacial Palace Resort, and then what kind of a friend would I be?"

Cora snorted again. "A dead one. Okay I'll quit. We should be there soon anyway."

I settled back in the wide, faux leather seat to concentrate on my breathing until Cora interrupted moments later.

"When do we meet Austin?"

Pressing my eyes closed, I finished releasing the deep breath in my lungs and answered for the fifth time, possibly the sixth since we took off. "Austin Cooper is—"

"Fucking hot as hell," Cora finished with a whoop.

"A *representative of the resort*. He's hired to look good, not be a male prostitute."

"He's doing a great job representing just by existing. And I don't expect him to charge. He should want this for free anyway."

I glanced over to catch my friend gesturing to her body. Trying not to roll my eyes, I drew another breath before continuing. "We get to go on an expedition with him, which I happen to be very excited about. It's one of the two reasons I even entered the contest. He's an expert at extreme sports and survival in harsh climates. Try not to get us slapped with a restraining order before then, okay?" I grabbed her arm, so she'd know I was serious.

"Fine." She frowned. "There'll be plenty of hot guys and gorgeous women. I'll save Austin for you."

"Ugh." I beat my skull back into the headrest. "I'm not here to date."

"You should be after the disaster of a *relationship* you just went through." She made air quotes around the word relationship.

"Daniel is a world-class—"

"Asshole? Dickhead?"

"Professor!" I whisper-shouted at her. "Honestly. We share an appreciation for the mythology surrounding native cultures."

"What you share*d*," she accented the D, "was a need to get laid while drowning in academia. The problem was that he took advantage."

"It was consensual." I bristled at her accusation, though I'd heard it from her before. It was just that it touched a nerve. I wished she would drop it since I'd broken up with my dissertation advisor a month ago. He'd understood.

Then again, he'd be in a pile of manure the size of Indiana if he said anything to the department, so I supposed he had little choice in the matter. And the thing that Cora didn't know was that technically, I initiated the entire thing. I needed Daniel if I was going to get a green light on my work, and since he'd grown leery based on the subject matter, I hit the fast forward button on what he'd been hinting at anyway. The attraction was mutual while my technical pursuits teetered on the edge of what many called pseudoscience. I cringed inwardly at the word. I'd prove them all wrong no matter what it took. It might be the 22nd century, but the patriarchy still thought they knew everything about the way the world worked.

The pilot's voice thankfully interrupted my thoughts and announced we'd be landing shortly. I leaned over Cora's seat and slid a finger across the glass, letting the sensor know to eliminate the tint. Instantly, the bright azure sky filled the floor length panel to her right, and a breathtaking scene infused me with excitement rather than nerves.

Below us, the crystalline land stretched out in undulating hills and mountains, punctuated by inlets of water so clear and still they could have been mirrors. White reflected everywhere against the bluest backdrop I could have imagined. And rising from the center of what felt like a vast untouched wonderland was what looked like a fairytale palace made of ice.

"I think I might've dressed inappropriately," Cora said, frowning out the window.

I elbowed her. "I told you that before we left. But it'll be fine. We enter directly into the resort, and it is climate controlled." I'd studied every article, website, and schematic available when I'd been informed I'd won the grand prize, all-expenses-paid trip.

During landing, my leg bounced spasmodically as my foot tapped the floor. I guessed I was anxious to get going. Now that I could see it for myself, the dream I'd had felt so much more like a silly nightmare induced by anxiety about finishing my dissertation. Well, that and probably all the Inuit monster lore I'd studied up on before coming. Now that I was here, I couldn't wait to explore the educational museum portion of the resort that held never before uncovered information about the local environment, as well as the Inuit culture, the closest native people to the unexplored interior we were about to inhabit for a month.

According to the website, there was even an Inuit teacher who offered classes on their culture. I couldn't believe my luck. It would be perfect for my dissertation material if they'd agree to an interview. And I couldn't help imagining Austin Cooper's expedition leading me to some new archeological discovery, like cave paintings, or even an *Adlet*, the Inuit version of a werewolf. It made my toes tingle to think about it.

A gentle tap was all I felt of the landing before we coasted between the icy walls of the compound. They seemed to purposely curve with points and texture that allowed the natural light to dance across them in a beautiful visual display. Bright white might have been what I'd expected, but what I saw were iridescent rainbows of undulating light that stole my breath.

The *oohs* and *ahhs* from the others on the plane confirmed I wasn't the only one. The Bennets had really put some design work into this place. Maybe someday I'd be able to afford a vacay to one of their other fantasy resorts. The Time Capsule Resort already occupied the top spot on my bucket list if they were to choose a destination like ancient Mayan or Incan times. Not that this was anything to sneeze at. The opportunity this would provide toward my studies was more than I could have hoped for.

Luck had truly found me, and I wasn't naïve enough to think I'd ever have another opportunity like this.

Time to buck up, Rosi. No hesitation or timidity on this trip. For the next month, I pledged to be more like Cora and jump at every opportunity given.

"Excuse me, Ms. Sanchez?"

I looked up into the eyes of the hostess who'd supplied Cora's many beverages and my one, barely touched hydropod. I was glad the water and container were both consumable and recyclable or I'd have felt guilty.

"Yes?" I glanced around at the other passengers as we glided to a stop so flawless I barely felt it.

"Ms. Bennet has asked that you remain seated until everyone else has had a chance to disembark."

Sweat coated my palms, and my heartrate kicked up a notch. "Is something wrong?"

"On the contrary!" The woman leaned down to reassure me with a pat on the shoulder. "She wishes to greet you herself. It's all part of your special trip."

I glanced to Cora, who shrugged.

"Ms. Fines?" The hostess said to Cora. "You can go on ahead. A member of the staff will escort you to your suite."

"I guess I'll meet you there?" I said, pleading with my eyes for Cora to insist on sticking by my side.

Instead, my best friend stood up and climbed over me to get to the aisle. "Sounds good."

And before I knew it, she was lost in the melee of those exiting the plane. The hostess, whose nametag still an inch from my face read "Brianna," stayed by me. She probably meant well, but I couldn't shake the feeling she was making sure I behaved by blocking my exit until the last person left.

Brianna raised a finger to her ear, receiving some sort of communication. She plastered on a smile and stepped back, sweeping an arm out to allow me passage.

"Right this way, Ms. Sanchez."

Swallowing down the panic that insisted on attacking me for no reason, I stood and wiped my hands on the legs of my jeans.

It's fine. Everything is fine. It was my mantra as I rounded the corner to the exit ramp.

But it wasn't fine because the first thing that greeted me was the roar of applause and chatter as lights flashed, stealing my vision with spots to the point I had to throw up an arm to shade my face.

"Now, now, let the poor thing off the plane. No flash, please." A woman's commanding voice silenced the crowd so I could recover enough to blink the world back into place.

My knees buckled at the sight of at least fifty news cameras hovering around the plane, and what I assumed were journalists to match. I reached out for something to prevent myself from going down and gripped an arm. A strong, warm arm.

One glance to my left showed I'd just latched onto none other than Cora's dream man, Austin Cooper himself.

2

ROSI

My eyes stretched wide as I took in Austin's beautiful face in detail, down to the blond stubble splattering his cheeks. The scent of earth grounded me as his soft gray eyes wrinkled in concern.

I was about to snatch my hand back when he covered it with his own, steadying me even as the sturdy thump of my own pulse eclipsed all other sound. His lips moved. He must've been speaking.

Another arm brushed my right side, and I turned to find a face I also recognized from the news vids. Up close, Owner and CEO of all the Fantasy Resorts, Nicole Bennet, was just as beautiful and powerful as she looked in the media in an Insta-fit suit of pseudo carbon fiber. For today she had altered the ensemble to dark-blue pants with matching blazer and a flowing silk looking tie. Clothing that could change color, fit, and shape like that cost enough to feed a family for half a year.

My head cleared as the same commanding voice I heard earlier came into focus. I wasn't surprised it belonged to Nicole.

"...warm welcome to our contest winner, Ms. Rosalind Sanchez. I'm sure you have many questions, but we don't want to overwhelm our guest. So we'll take three."

Three questions? For me? I never agreed to this.

As if sensing my distress, Austin's hand gave a reassuring squeeze. God, it was huge, completely dwarfing mine. I wondered if there were other parts of him just as big...

Oh my Lord, I must've been panicking worse than I thought.

Nicole pointed to somewhere in the masses as a hovercam slid close, angling its lens down toward where Austin and I connected.

"Rosalind, what's it like to win the vacation of your dreams?" a woman's velvety voice asked.

My throat felt like the Sahara climbed in my mouth. I licked my lips, trying to form words. "It—it—it's great." Oh, Lord, I sounded like an incompetent idiot. *Great?*

"What are you looking forward to most?" a man asked as I considered the plethora of adjectives I could have conjured instead.

"Forward to?" I repeated, blinded momentarily by a flash of light.

Austin squeezed my hand again.

"Austin," I said out loud, glancing at him. Then I stopped, mouth hanging open with the realization I'd just insinuated that I was most looking forward to him specifically. Not his expedition.

His cheeks darkened slightly as he grinned out at the audience, pointedly not making eye contact with me. "Who can blame her?" he asked, and a resounding bout of laughter echoed off the icy walls.

Fuckity fuck fuck fuck. "No I—"

"One more," Nicole said, indicating somewhere in the midst of the crowd.

"Rumor is you're working on your...doctorate?" The man hesitated as though he might have gotten the information wrong. I nodded as my stomach curdled. "In anthropology at USC. Think you might make any interesting discoveries while you're here?"

Forcing down the dry bulge in my throat, I prepared to launch into my field of interest and mention the classes and museum I was so intrigued by, thinking that might redeem me to some extent.

A woman spoke first. "Let us know if you discover whether Austin wears boxers or tighty-whities."

The crowd erupted into hysterics once again, and my mouth snapped shut. The embarrassment was all encompassing as Austin patted my hand before letting go. I desired to melt into the ground and let the ice swallow me whole but found myself trapped on a stage, stupefied face likely broadcast on holos worldwide. I'd be famous for being the inarticulate, sex-crazed imbecile who embarrassed Austin Cooper. *Yay me.*

"I'm sure Ms. Sanchez is tired from her trip. Let's all give her some space to enjoy herself, shall we?" Nicole clapped and, in what felt like a single blink, the crowd dispersed.

The smile melted off her face as she turned toward me, sizing me up.

I cleared my throat. "Sorry, I would have prepared but I had no idea—"

Nicole waved her hand, cutting me off. "That was perfect. Now every young woman watching will imagine herself here instead, fantasizing about how she could impress Austin better."

I could find literally no good response to that.

"I hope you enjoy your stay, Ms. Sanchez. Let us know if there's anything you need." Nicole nodded and walked away, her heels clicking against the clear floor.

My shoulders sagged as I finally relaxed only to realize Austin was still there.

"Oh shit." The words slipped out. Apparently, my mouth had plenty of good ones when they were uncalled for and none when they were.

I buried my face in my hands, took a deep breath, and tried again. "Sorry. I didn't realize you were still there. I'm not like this normally. I swear." *Stop talking, Rosi.*

Austin chuckled and crossed his arms, displaying his corded mountain climbing muscles like a gilded statue. "No need to apologize. You were pretty much ambushed just then."

I sighed, relieved that he understood. "Seriously! A little warning would've been nice. I'm not great with public speaking, though I guess that was obvious."

Austin's smile inched wider, making his eyes scrunch up in the corners. "You did *great*."

His emphasis on the last word made me cringe. I deserved that.

"No really," he said, reaching out and letting his hand graze my arm. "All jokes aside, it's tough when you're under a spotlight like that. It took me at least a year to learn to master my composure. There's an old joke about picturing the crowd in their underwear, and I'm not saying to try it because you may end up in hysterics and look worse."

I couldn't help but laugh.

He answered with a grin far more genuine than the one he'd had at the press conference. "Anyway, I'm sure you gave Ms. Bennet exactly what she wanted at the very least. If I get wind of any more surprise press conferences, I'll try to send you a heads-up. Nice to meet you by the way." He held out a hand, and I shook it.

"Thanks for being so gracious. I don't really think you're the best part of the tri—" I caught myself too late, and he dropped my hand, raising his eyebrows while pouting. "What I mean is, I'm looking forward to our expedition."

"Same here. Do you have any training or experience? It's good to know what I'm going in with."

Heat rushed to my face. "I regularly go to the gym on campus. But hiking is about as outdoorsy as I get in LA. When I was a teenager, I loved skiing and camping though. I used to vacation in Colorado or Oregon with my family, so at least I know what snow is."

"That's something," Austin said, leading the way out of the cavernous landing area and toward the arched tunnels that presumably led into the resort.

"I study native mythologies, and I'm hoping to discover some-thing about the source of some of the Inuit myths." It was a politically correct way of saying I was out to prove the existence of cryptids.

Austin glanced sideways at me as we passed by multiple icicle-framed tunnel entrances, each at least ten feet tall and milling with people, headed toward the sound of rushing water. "I can't promise any more than ice and snow for miles."

As well designed as this place was, the lack of winter's freezing air made the whole thing feel wrong. I shouldn't have been comfortable in a T-shirt and jeans, yet here I was. The stinging cold that hit my exposed skin on my occasional skiing trip was MIA. The incredible landscape outside of the AC glass, filled with stark contrasts of pristine snow, crystal blue skies, and sparkling ice that promised the full arctic experience reassured me I'd truly landed in the Tundra.

"I understand there are no guarantees. But if there are any real ice caves or hidden crevices out there..." I let my voice trail off, gesturing out at the picturesque view where a shadow wavered far on the snowy horizon. Probably a polar bear or something, I supposed.

"Glad to hear you are adventurous," Austin said and winked.

We rounded a corner, and a massive space came into view, stealing my attention. At least six stories tall, the main courtyard's centerpiece rushed over stepped rock ledges in crashing waves. The waterfall foamed into bubbling white froth at the bottom that sloshed up the clear fence at least as high as my head. The whole thing was a good quarter-mile wide as well, circled in snowcapped boulders of varying heights.

"That's amazing," I said, once again unable to find better words.

"Amazing but not exactly accurate unless global warming had managed to destroy the glaciers and environmental stabilizers hadn't been invented." Austin crossed his arms, glaring at the spectacle like it was a mouse masquerading as a lion.

I nodded in response. "Good point. But it is pretty to look at."

"Just because something's pretty doesn't mean it's productive or even truthful."

Austin's comment stung. Of course he was right. But was he talking about the waterfall or something else?

"So I don't suppose you know where my room would be?" I asked, exhaustion catching up to me as I glanced around at the seemingly endless shops, restaurants, and streams of people filing in and out amongst them.

"Check your wristcom for the room number," Austin said.

Again, something simple I should've thought of myself. Good thing I wasn't trying to impress him or I'd practically be in tears by this point.

I glanced at my wrist. "Suite 600," I reported.

"Right next door. Come on, I'll walk you up." Austin waved me toward what appeared to be an escalator made of ice, though I knew it couldn't be real because of not only the comfortable temperature but the risk of guests slipping. Inside, the gears spun in a hypnotic dance, rolling the steps upward in a smooth motion. Beside it, more boulders stacked in a step-like formation reaching for the enormous domed ceiling. The ultra-thin, ultra-strong AC glass was so clear it looked as though nothing stood between the bright sky and us. Obviously it did, or we'd be frozen solid without so much as a jacket.

"Are those real rocks?" I asked, leaning over the railing to touch a small pile of snow on one nearly horizontal area the size of my arm. The cold, wet sensation made my fingertip sting as I stared at it in surprise.

"Yes. The snow is too. It's kept the right temperature with some sort of additive."

"Is it dangerous?" I asked, sniffing my freezing finger.

Austin laughed. "No. All part of the meteorologic tech that helped stabilize the environment seventy years ago. I thought you were a doctoral student, Ms. Sanchez?"

I glared at him, wiping my hand on my jeans. "I am. In anthropology, not meteorology or chemistry. And my name is Rosi."

We stepped off the escalator, and Austin gestured to an enormous tube that looked like it was carved directly out of a block of ice. A closer look revealed a completely see-through, steadily moving ramp that led upward. I hesitated, glancing over at a second tube down the hall.

"It's kind of a cross between an elevator and escalator. This way." Austin gestured for me to go first.

Stepping inside, and finding no rail to hold on to, I folded my arms across the sasquatch art on my chest instead. It was my favorite T-shirt and read, "Bigfoot believes in me."

The ramp rose smoothly at the perfect pace somewhere between "get me there already" and "take your time and enjoy the scenery."

Austin spoke without looking at me. "Floor six."

The entire tube lifted and angled itself in another direction, apparently readjusting so that it would let us out on the sixth floor. It was freaky flying through the air, but also smooth and somehow secure. I'd almost forgotten Austin was with me until he spoke.

"I hope you have a lovely stay, Rosi. I'll be meeting with you next week to discuss the details of our excursion."

If that wasn't a dismissal, I wasn't sure what was. For some reason, it irked me more than it should have, and I turned to focus on him, tugging on his arm to get him to look at me.

"Listen, Austin. This is going to be a really awkward experience unless we start over. I honestly didn't mean what I said earlier. I have absolutely no interest in you in that way. What I do have an interest in is this once-in-a-lifetime chance to go out there and explore." I stopped short of saying "search for things no one's ever captured indisputable evidence of." There was no point in sounding crazier than I already did today.

Austin tilted his head like he was looking at me for the first time. He opened his mouth, and the ramp beneath our feet jolted, knocking me off balance. He grabbed me so that we gripped each other's arms and held me steady until I righted myself.

"What was that?" I asked, staring down through the nearly invisible material at the drop of at least four stories below us. I sincerely hoped no one on the resort had a fear of heights.

"I'm not sure. Are you okay?" Austin asked.

Maybe it was my imagination, but his voice felt kinder than it had so far, more personal.

"I am. Computer, why are we stopped?" I asked, letting go of his hold.

The lack of an answer amped up my anxiety, and I glanced at Austin, hoping he'd have an explanation.

"Computer," Austin said in a voice so commanding it made me jump instead of feeling better.

About to full-on panic, I focused on the wall of rock and ice through the window to my left. Austin drew in a couple of deep breaths. I was about to make a joke about him climbing the rest of the way up and carrying me on his back when the ramp whirred and glided into motion as though nothing had happened.

When we reached the top moments later, I stepped out gratefully onto solid ground. "What do you think that was?" I asked when he paused in the hall, searching my face with his stormy-eyed gaze.

"I'm not sure, but I will let Nicole know. Do me a favor, and if anything else like that happens, tell me?"

Why would I tell him? Wasn't he just the face of the resort, not the mechanic?

"Rosi?" he asked, his voice a low, rumbling tone that made my panties wet. Holy shit, he could say my name and I'd come running any day.

I nodded in agreement and swallowed back whatever damning words wanted to escape my lips. I'd just told him I wasn't interested in him like that. He'd think I was psycho if he didn't already. And if

I wanted him to make this expedition more than just a show, I needed him to trust me.

"I'll see you later then," he said with a dazzling smile. But it was the fake one he'd used with the newsvids. My heart sunk.

"You said you'd take me to my room," I said to stop him from leaving.

"I did." He gestured to the double doors beside us. Six hundred was carved in the thick white ice in front. "You, uh, use your wristcom as a key," he explained, waving his arm in front of me.

"Right." The embarrassment had to have shown on my face as I lifted my own and waved it in front of the doors, which promptly slid open.

I watched him walk down the hall to the next of what must be enormous suites and disappear into his room with a wave that made me want to follow him like a puppy. Instead, I pressed my forehead into the icy surface of the entryway to cool me down. This was going to be a long vacation.

3

ROSI

FORGET EXPLORING THE ROOM. THE FIRST THING I SAW WHEN I looked up was Cora in my face.

"Was that Austin's voice I heard? Tell me he's grabbing a bottle of champagne and coming back to join us." She peered around my shoulder, and I had to move to catch hold of her before she ran up and down the halls screaming his name.

"Settle down, chica." I marched her backward into the suite and relaxed when I heard the doors swish shut. "Yes, it was Austin. No, he's not coming over. Yes, you will meet him next week when we plan the excursion."

Cora flopped down onto an exceptionally fluffy-looking, white sofa with a long, curved backrest that made it look like a snowy mountain range or perhaps glaciers. "Party pooper."

Frowning, I took in the rest of the luxurious accommodations. It was all glass and white. Several oversized, high-tech massage pods that resembled white beanbags made me suddenly aware of the tension in my shoulders. Though I'd never tried one, I understood the principle of using electromagnetic fields to read a sitter's brainwaves and temperature and respond with ideal movement and pressure. Glass end tables, with what I assumed to be faux icicles dripping from their sides, were also interspersed around the room. The icicle theme continued throughout and along the counter and table edges as well as framing the wall-sized window with a spectacular view of the landscape.

"Beautiful isn't it?" Cora asked as the tundra drew me in like a magnet. Before I knew it, my nose pressed up against the AC glass.

"It's breathtaking. I can't believe I'm here. Pinch me. Ow!" I shouldn't have said it. I knew better from previous experience.

Cora laughed and spun around, making her skirt fly out around her in a rainbow whirl that stood out spectacularly against all the white. "Believe it, baby!"

I couldn't have stopped the giddy laughter if I'd tried. This was amazing despite the news conference ambush and Austin's weirdness.

"So I'm thinking we use the old scarf-on-the-door method if one of us has a visitor," Cora said, pacing the length of the room as I stared out at the glass-like surface of the fjord and the tops of the glaciers rising into the cobalt sky. "I realize there's no doorknob, but we can stick it between the sliders. I don't think the sensors will pick it up if it's thin. Okay, maybe I already tested it."

A small and sudden motion outside the window caught my eye, and I narrowed my gaze, straining to see into the shadows between the crags of some snow-covered rocks.

"Unless of course Austin is over. In which case, if you don't mind sharing, I'm okay with a ménage."

About to chalk it up to a reflection, I relaxed slightly, and it happened again. Something dark, almost like a shadow shifted, changing the shape of the darkness—like a blackness creeping slowly toward the surface of the water.

I didn't imagine that.

"We just have to set some ground rules ahead of time," Cora continued behind me as a tiny ripple stirred the water's mirror-like surface, which was even crazier since I was certain the water was frozen solid.

"Get the binoculars!" I shouted, unwilling to take my eyes off it.

"Well, that's one ground rule I'm not sure about," she said.

I waved her off, staring intently at the spot. "No. Now. I saw something. Grab them from my backpack."

"Oh! On it."

Ten seconds later she shoved the small black bit of metal into my hand. I slipped it over my eyes and it clung to my face, automatically adjusting the picture of the area where I'd been staring. Cora's arm brushed against my side as she crammed in next to me to look.

"What is it?"

"I'm not sure yet. But there's definitely something out there. And it affected the water without actually touching it."

Cora hummed softly. "Directing energy at a source? Maybe it has telekinesis."

We might disagree on some things, but Cora was my best friend in part because she believed me without question, when not another soul would. Not even my parents. And for that I trusted her completely, even being open to things *I* thought previously impossible.

"Or invisibility?" I suggested, excitement bubbling up in my gut like lava. "If it could somehow cloak itself then that would explain a lot about why some of these creatures aren't easy to spot. That would be quite an evolutionary boon."

After a full ten minutes of nothing further happening, I reluctantly removed the binoculars and shoved them in my pocket with a sigh.

Cora had given up far earlier and currently meditated cross-legged on a massage pod with her hands positioned in a mudra and her eyes closed. I'd have to make sure to tell her explicitly I did not plan on any threesomes when she came out of it. Otherwise, she'd assume no answer was a yes.

I sprawled across the sofa, staring up at the glass dome of the ceiling into the perfect topaz sky, dotted with the occasional puff as white as the snow below. Apparently, we were on the top floor of the resort, though I'd noticed another inner dome above the central area ringed by the floors. This really was luxury beyond my wildest dreams.

Believing Cora's assertion fate had won me this trip was difficult to swallow. So was her other idea—that I manifested the result when I entered. That would have involved me believing I'd win, and that was certainly not the case. But whatever it was, even sheer dumb luck, I was grateful, and I wasn't going to waste a second of this amazing opportunity.

The cushions beneath me were as plush as they looked, and my eyelids drooped as I stared up at the drifting wisps of clouds. The muscles in my back and shoulders relaxed, and I sank deeper into the softness cradling me, feeling like I was floating along with the white puffs above. It had been a long time since I'd gotten some sleep because of that damn nightmare. I'd explore the museum as soon as I caught a quick catnap.

My chest burned as I ran, the scenery jolting with each crunch of snow beneath my boots. Just a little farther—it wouldn't want to lose its camouflage. The hair on the back of my neck stood on end, rubbing against the thermal material of my shirt. I could feel the creature bearing down on me, closer with each stretch of its long legs.

"Run!" The voice was Austin's I realized, even as the awareness that I was dreaming seeped into the moment. Still, the monster didn't stop. I pumped my muscles harder, propelling myself forward as the vision of the resort loomed closer and larger before me.

I was going to make it.

But I didn't. The weight of the beast knocked me to the ground, more unforgiving than I'd imagined. Heat seared through my parka as its body pinned me there, breath reeking of a fresh kill as it snarled near my ear.

Tears streamed down my face, freezing against my skin, and then I was free. I rolled to see what happened and found Austin wrestling with it. The thing moved too quickly for me to see more than a flash of razor-sharp claws or matted hair. And before I could focus, before I could scream, hot, red blood exploded over my face, blinding me to all except Austin's arm hanging limply across the snow.

"No!" I woke sitting up, the word still echoing around me. Sweat soaked my T-shirt, and my lungs still burned like I'd really been running.

I glanced around, making sure I was in my room as the panic subsided. Swallowing, I slid my feet onto the floor and pressed my face into my hands.

"Fuck." It was the same as the other night, but even more detailed. And it felt so real.

As I drew my hands down and away, I glanced around the room again. No Cora. A quick peek at my wristcom told me she'd left a holomessage, so I flicked it on. A tiny version of her filled the space between me and my wrist.

"You needed some sleep, so I decided to go for a swim. Come down and join me if you're bored." She blew me a kiss and disappeared back into the thin band.

Right, sleep, the thing I may never do again.

Locating the bathroom and some supplies, I decided a nice hot shower would help wash away some of the residual fear. The walk-in ice cave shower with seven heads certainly was luxurious. The hot spray and vanilla-scented wash relaxed me back into a positive mood. This was what happened when one studied monsters for a living, I reasoned. And the purpose for Austin being in the dream was obviously because I'd just met him. It wasn't a portent of the future or even a subconscious hint that I liked him. Nope, it wasn't.

By the time I dried my hair and pulled on my *Know what really gets my goat?* Chupacabra shirt, I felt like myself again. And that excitement from earlier began to fizz like the foam at the bottom of the waterfall below. But I had more important things to explore than the pool.

I hesitated at the top of the downward tube but decided that at least walking down the ramp six floors would be easier than walking up if it stopped moving and got on. Fortunately though, nothing malfunctioned, and I reached the main level without incident.

Checking my wristcom for directions, I made my way past the myriad of tourist attractions, including a holo adventure featuring polar bears and reindeer. Finally, I reached my destination—the museum I'd been so eager to visit.

The doors slid shut behind me, erasing the noise of the busy resort and allowing me a breath of relief. The smell that always accompanied institutions of learning settled over me, something akin to the musty scent of old-fashioned paper books that spoke of wisdom collected over years. Smiling, I inhaled deeply and glanced around at the various exhibition rooms, each labeled with a neon-blue holosign dripping icicles.

Only a few other people shuffled around, each engrossed in reading the signage or investigating objects. My gaze settled on the room titled, *The People of Greenland*. The clear glass delineating every other alcove was absent here. Instead, the whole area was hidden behind a tinted version that blacked out any view of the interior. Curious, I strode forward, the sliders opening as I approached.

The full-sized holo of a man and woman flickered along the darkened back wall of the space while sprawled on either side of them were glass cases holding various pieces of history. I was immediately drawn toward the smiling couple at the center, and as if it were mutual, the man turned toward me, eyes crinkling at the corners in welcome.

"That's my husband."

The voice to my left made me jump and throw a hand against my chest.

"Sorry, didn't mean to startle you."

I turned to find the actual version of the other half of the holo couple before me. But in real life, she stood a few inches shorter and was a bit rounder. The lines tattooed on her chin stood out starker as well, drawing my gaze down toward her mouth.

"I hadn't realized anyone else was here," I said offering my hand. "I'm Rosi."

"Nice to meet you, Rosi. I'm Ila." Her hand was warm and rough in mine as she shook with strength.

I felt my smile broaden, genuinely happy that luck found me again. A one-on-one with a member of the Inuit culture was more than I'd hoped for on day one. "I'm actually a doctoral student. I'm studying First People's cultures and mythology."

Ila laughed and released my hand. "Well if you want to see an animal skin kayak, it's over there by Nanuq."

"I'm sorry, did you just say there was a polar bear here?" I asked, scanning the room.

This time her laugh was so boisterous, Ila nearly doubled over. "You speak the language a bit, huh? Good for you. No. That's my husband's name. Though he looks a little like a polar bear with dark skin. He's round enough."

I grabbed a curl from the side of my head and twisted it around a finger, desperate to stick it in my mouth along with the foot already there. But Ila patted me on the back and guided me over to the opposite side of the holos instead.

"Here's the pottery shards from my ancestors as well as some well-preserved *kamik*. Those are the—"

"The soft boots. Also called mukluks," I finished for her.

She narrowed her eyes at me, studying me a bit closer. "So you've done your homework."

It was impossible to tell if she was appreciative or felt like I was a know-it-all who barely scratched the surface and acted like I understood her people. I hoped that wasn't how I'd come off.

"I...did as much cursory research as I could before the trip, but I'm hoping you can help me learn more of the important details. I know I'll never understand things the way I would if I'd grown up here myself and experienced things firsthand, but I want to get as far as I can toward remedying that."

She smiled back at me, hand on her hip. "Honestly? I thought this would be the easiest job ever. Didn't imagine I'd actually have people coming to my classes to *learn* things. I figured some kids maybe who'd want to do crafts and make some dolls."

"Guess it was obvious I was interested in the class, huh?" I asked with a chuckle.

"Hey, I may as well earn my paycheck. Come on by tomorrow morning." She gestured to a door in the corner of the room that would have been easy to miss. "That's my office. We can talk in more detail, and you can ask me whatever you want."

"What about Nanuq?" I asked, glancing around for her actual husband.

"He's at home. He talked to the *angakukk* who told him this was cursed ground." She shrugged despite the shocking statement. "He believes everything the man says. I suspect it's because he doesn't trust the Bennets' money or motives. But I don't care where it comes from. I won't say no to a good paycheck."

So the local shaman warned her off but she still came. *Interesting.*

"I definitely want to know more about the *angakukk*," I said, making a mental note.

"You said you study mythology?" Ila asked, adjusting her brightly-colored sweater.

I wondered briefly if the traditional clothing was her own idea or Nicole's and frowned before nodding my head.

"I've never been much into the myths, but I know them. If Nanuq was here, he'd give you an earful for sure."

"I appreciate whatever you can give me in the way of information." Before I could ask about any specific myths or creatures, a young boy ran up to Ila.

"Do you have any toys?" he asked.

His parents rushed over, apologies spilling from their mouths. Ila glanced at me with a wink as she pointed the boy toward the small figurines in the corner. Looked like I'd have to organize my thoughts and ask more the next day when I met privately with her.

As I exited the room, something caught my eye in a small show-case in the corner. It was a tower of stones backlit with a placard that read: *Inuksuk. These stone arrangements, often in the shape of figures, are left to mark a specific geographic spot.* Before leaving, I looked to the other side of the door and froze. Staring back at me from that display case was a small, mishappen figurine. It seemed to have a dark glow surrounding it.

I inched closer and shivered as its empty eyes bore into me, its oversized head elongated like a ceremonial mask of some sort. It looked like other totems I'd seen, except it somehow felt...wrong, and I couldn't quite place why. A glance at the description only made things worse. *Tupilaq. Made of animal bones or parts, sometimes of deceased children, the tupilaq is created by an angakukk to seek revenge on someone. Now these figures are often made as art or souvenirs for others. This particular one is believed to have been carved in recent years by an angakukk in the hopes of sending the spirit of the tupilaq after an outcast.*

No wonder it gave me the heebie-jeebies. It was basically a curse, or worst-case scenario, a golem made for revenge instead of protection.

Not wanting to spend any more time looking at the object, I took a quick picture with my wristcom and headed out of the museum and back up to my room.

With any luck, Cora would be finished with her swim and ready for dinner and a few drinks. It had been a long day, and if I didn't loosen up and get my mind off things, it would be a *tupilaq* that visited me in my nightmares.

4

ROSI

WHEN MORNING ROLLED AROUND AND I STUMBLED OUT OF THE bedroom, coffee was all that was on my mind. I nearly tripped over Cora meditating on the floor in a lotus position on my way to the kitchen.

"Ugh. How can you be up this early?" I asked, pressing buttons on the autobot to order my cup the way I liked it—cream, no sugar.

Cora popped one eye open and stared at me. "It's almost noon, standard time, and you look like one of your monsters."

Inhaling the medicinal scent of coffee, I let her comment roll off of me then took a sip. "Don't insult the sasquatch."

Cora laughed, opened both eyes, and stood to stretch. "So what's the plan for today? Want to go get massages? Take a ride on a dog sled?"

"The Inuit call them *qamutik*. But no. I have an appointment to interview the local expert," I said, already thinking ahead to the notebook filled with questions waiting on my nightstand.

"Puppies cute. Rosi use big words," Cora said, ordering herself a chai tea.

I flicked her on the shoulder and guzzled some more nectar of the gods. "You can go see the pups. Let me know how it is. Maybe I can do that with you later. I do want to get used to going outside a little at a time."

Cora shrugged. "Your choice. I know you're excited, but we're supposed to be on vacay, not working." She didn't wait for my response as she headed for the shower, shedding layers of pajamas as she went.

Sighing, I picked up her laundry trail after I heard the water running and tossed the clothes on her bed. If she wanted to leave a mess, she could do it in her own space.

My wristcom buzzed just as I began sorting out what I wanted to wear for my meeting. When I checked, I found Austin Cooper's name flashing in gold letters across the screen. Curious, I twisted my wrist to answer, and his figure bloomed into the air before me.

"Hi, Rosi. It's Austin."

"I gathered," I said, amused at his awkwardness. "What's up? Did you want to meet to discuss the expedition early?" That would have made an ideal plan for the afternoon.

"Not yet," he said, brushing a hand back through his sun-kissed mane of hair. "I told Nicole about the issue on the tubes yesterday, and she wanted me to let you know that an unexpected sun flare messed with the tech. She said not to worry about it. They're working on it." He shuffled one foot and glanced to the left, frowning.

Why was he being so jittery and awkward? That wasn't how Mr. Master of Surprise News Conferences came off yesterday at all. "Austin, is...everything okay?" I asked.

"What? Yeah, why? Of course it is. How's your stay so far? Do anything fun?"

Well, that was evasive. "I have a meeting with Ila, the Inuit expert. I'd love to chat with you about specific things to keep an eye out for on our expedition."

"Yeah, yeah. When we meet next week. Definitely." The figure of Austin floating over my wrist flickered and sparked before going out.

"What the hell?" I shook my wrist to make sure nothing caught fire.

"Definitely lying," Cora said from behind me.

"Why? About what?" I turned to find her towel drying her hair.

"Who knows? I didn't even hear the convo, just got the vibe loud and clear." She flipped her head back up and shook out her wild locks.

I stared at my inactive wristband and frowned. It was weird. The only thing he'd said was some excuse for the tech failing yesterday. *Why would he randomly call me for that only to lie about it?*

"You could go ask him why he lied," Cora offered with a wink. "He'll either tell you or distract you with sex. Either way you win."

"Or he could think I'm crazy and refuse to take me on the expedition." I tossed my *Abominable seems a bit harsh* T-shirt on the bed with my black jeans and headed for the shower.

"Then you distract him with sex!" she called after me as I disappeared into the bathroom.

Something was off, I just didn't know what. I chewed on a piece of hair as I readied the waterfall of warmth. I never could resist a mystery. Maybe confronting Austin was the best way forward. I'd long ago discovered that annoying people often got you further than being polite. And though I didn't want to piss him off enough to ruin my expedition, if I could get him to open up to me, I might just be able to convince him to help truly guide me to something worthwhile in the arctic tundra outside the resort.

As the hot water streamed over me, I let my mind wander. When I'd first met Daniel, I'd been in awe of his intelligence and position. He was where I wanted to be—honored as an expert in his field, and he'd earned it. He was kind, funny if a bit nerdy, and so smart it sometimes intimidated me. He was young for a professor and hung out with us grad students too often. When I caught him watching me one night over beers and discussions about some new findings from a professor in Chicago about Ancient Greek weapons, he blushed so hard I worried he'd faint.

He never tried anything, though I knew he wanted to. And I never encouraged it, until our meeting about my dissertation proposal.

Alone in his office, I'd gripped the edge of his worn desk too tightly to prevent my hands from shaking. I remembered telling him my proposed topic and him laughing in response like he assumed it was a joke. When I didn't join in, he sobered up pretty quickly, but that sinking feeling I knew so well had already taken hold. All my life I had been ridiculed and dismissed as a silly girl when I *knew* the truth. I couldn't let him stand in my way. I had to convince him.

We argued for a good hour about the scientific probabilities and lack of evidence regarding the existence of cryptids—animals that shouldn't exist but that so many believed did. I explained that it wasn't just our culture. They'd been talked about since ancient times all over the world. I knew I had lost when he glanced at the time on his old-fashioned watch.

I made my decision in the space of a single, desperate heartbeat. I'd never thrown myself at anyone before, but I'd read enough romance novels to know how it worked.

When I broke up with him, I did it because it hadn't felt fair to lead him on anymore. I tried to love him, I honestly did. But the feelings just wouldn't come no matter how sweet he was. I'd never been secure enough in our relationship to tell him the truth about *why* I wanted to study what I wanted to study. Maybe that was what had prompted me to break it off.

Whatever the reason, my heart wasn't in it. And it scared me more than a little bit that that same heart wanted to go wild and beat its way out of my body when I got close to a man I had just met. It was like it knew something I didn't yet—like it had recognized something in Austin that my brain had yet to uncover.

Maybe it was just karma. If I fell for Austin and couldn't have him, I guess I'd have gotten a taste of what Daniel must've felt.

It didn't matter if I set myself up for heartbreak. I had to risk spending time with Austin if I wanted to get the most out of my expedition into the center of Greenland. Because that was what mattered, and I couldn't lose sight of that.

5

AUSTIN

T<small>HIS WAS NOT PART OF MY JOB DESCRIPTION.</small>

The resort owner and boss, Nicole, had seemed downright scared out of her wits when I told her about the tubes. I honestly hadn't thought much of it at the time, just felt like it would be something I'd want to know if I had a brand-new luxury resort. At least that was what I thought until the color drained from her face and she fell into the chair behind her. I knew it wasn't me either, because her boyfriend rushed to her side and whispered in her ear for a good minute at least.

As if to make the situation worse, when my pulse revved with worry, the lights blinked. Good thing I wasn't superstitious. But Nicole turned even whiter, if that were possible.

Then she asked me to give Rosi some bullshit story about a solar flare causing issues, which I didn't think she'd bought. I wouldn't have either. But Nicole looked so fucking scared, I couldn't say no. *How do I get myself into this shit?* I was supposed to stay calm under all circumstances. It was what I had spent years studying. It was how I had made it out of scrapes in the harshest conditions that should've been the end of me.

I'd taken on mountain lions, avalanches, and volcanoes. But

when it came to people? That shit messed me up. And now I had to meet with Rosi next week to discuss this excursion. I didn't know how to explain to her that it was not about searching for ancient civilizations or whatever it was she thought in that gorgeous head of hers. I didn't want to disappoint her with the truth, but I couldn't make it into more than it was designed to be—a four-hour excursion in a hellipod, taking in the land within two miles of the resort, and only a bit of walking in the tundra to snap a few vids or holos. I suspected that wasn't what Rosi had in mind.

Now I had to sustain Nicole's weird charade and keep the contest winner happy, which was part of my job description, without changing the script.

Breathe, Austin.

I counted in my head as I filled my lungs with air. I watched in my mind as I filled my body with light, chasing out the dark energy with the exhale that came on three. I'd learned it from a Tibetan Monk on one of my first climbs. It had saved my life more than once.

But as I pulled in a second breath, Rosi's face surfaced in my head instead of the energy I expected. The dimple in her left cheek deepened as she smiled mischievously, like she had when she'd reached out to touch the snow on the rocks.

The enthusiasm and energy she had for her studies was palpable, but her expectations were off the charts.

Damn, this was not working. It didn't help that the vision in my head expanded to include her whole body, which had been nearly impossible to ignore at the press conference when she came off the plane. I'd expected a middle-aged soccer mom, not a hot twenty-something who made my skin tingle when she grabbed my arm. I hadn't had sex in a whole year, since before my volcano surfing trip on the Big Island. It had been one event after another, and between prepping my body and mind for the increasingly difficult and deadly challenges, I hadn't had time to socialize, much less fuck.

But damn if Rosi didn't remind me of that every moment since stepping foot off that plane and into Nicole's marketing stunt. I couldn't pursue her though. She was forbidden fruit—the contest winner. If I were accused of seducing her, it would cause a public scandal. No way the Bennets would pay me after that. Worse, they'd pull the sponsorship they promised me for the first Space Games on their Big Bang Resort next year. I wanted that more than anything. I'd be among the first people to do a space hike through the adjoining asteroid field.

I drew in another deep breath and pushed the vision of Rosi's smooth caramel skin from my mind. No point wondering if it tasted as sweet as it looked because I'd never know. All I had to do was avoid her for the rest of the week, focus on only business when I met with her about the excursion, and keep us both safe outside for a few hours, more than half of which were on a hellipod. *Easy.*

My wristcom buzzed, and a small holo of Nicole popped up.

"Yes, boss?" I asked, hoping the misery wasn't obvious in my voice.

If she heard it, she ignored it.

"Get dressed for the weather and go grab Ms. Sanchez. We'll be taking publicity vids and holos outside at the playground in twenty minutes."

"That doesn't give us much time," I protested, standing.

"It's part of your job, Mr. Cooper."

"But it's not part of Rosi's. She's supposed to be able to enjoy a free vacation." I didn't add that I wanted to stay as far away from her as possible for propriety's sake.

"Rosi huh? Act like it's an invitation from you. Honestly, Mr. Cooper, I don't think you know your own power when it comes to the opposite sex. She's clearly smitten. Just use that to our advantage. Something tells me you wouldn't mind all that much."

"With all due respect, Ms. Bennet, I didn't sign up for this to manipulate people's emotions." I fisted my hand at my side, pressing down the anger and indignation that threatened to break through.

Nicole sighed and tossed her hair, which disappeared for a moment outside of the sphere of the holo. "I'm not asking you to do anything untoward, Mr. Cooper. I'm simply suggesting you look at this as an opportunity to have a good time with someone you're clearly interested in learning more about. Twenty minutes."

The figure disintegrated, and I lowered my arm. I didn't have much time, and if I didn't get Rosi, she'd be dragged out there by Nicole's people, making things much worse. And Nicole wasn't wrong about wanting to get to know Rosi better. Maybe this wouldn't be so terrible, considering it was sanctioned by the boss. I just couldn't take it any further than that—not with her. Not with anyone. It was an ugly truth I'd been ignoring because years had passed since I'd been forced to take a good hard look at it. I could risk my own life all I wanted, but not someone else's, never again, especially someone I might care about.

I already had one death on my conscience, and I couldn't survive a repeat experience.

Sara's face hadn't haunted my dreams in almost a year, but it seemed my penance wouldn't be that easy. I already felt something for Rosi, which was more than I should have allowed. There was just an energy about the woman that seemed to slice through my shields like they were made of vapor.

Maybe, I thought as I threw on some jeans, *this playground thing will help me get her out of my system before this goes too far.*

6

ROSI

THE KNOCK AT THE DOOR WAS BEYOND UNEXPECTED, BUT SEEING Austin on the other side, unmistakable even beneath his puffy hood and the balaclava tugged down below his chin, was downright shocking after our conversation earlier.

"Um, hi," I said as I felt Cora pop over my shoulder.

"Hi." Austin raised a gloved hand in a wave. "Remember how I said I'd give you a heads-up about any more ambushes by the press? Well get your gear on because we have to be outside in ten minutes. Sorry."

"That's not much of a heads-up," I said, panic starting to set in. I was sure I'd read all the fine print.

"I literally just found out," he said, shifting his weight back and forth from one leg to the other. "Don't worry. I can do most of the talking if you want. But I think they mainly want vids of us on the playground."

"Playground? As in swings?" I laughed.

"No, as in snowballs, sledding, and bunny hills." Austin smiled, and his bright white teeth showed against his golden, tanned skin.

My stomach tightened. Why was he so damned irresistible? It made me mad, mostly at myself for allowing any physical reaction.

But also at him for being so cagey and lying to me earlier. "What if I refuse to go?"

Austin frowned and stopped shifting, as if he hadn't considered a woman turning down any offer of his. That pissed me off even more.

"Why would you?" Cora asked, shoving my parka in my hands. "You're here to have fun, and what's more fun than sledding?"

Traitor. I tried to silently call her out with my eyes. But she only grinned back and tossed her hair, flirting with Austin as she turned her attention to him. For some reason, that upset me even more.

"If she's not going, I will," she said with a wink and a little shimmy of her shoulders.

"Fine I'll go!" I pushed by her, pulling on my gloves. "Stop making Austin uncomfortable and get my boots."

We didn't say much on the walk to the playground. Two sad tweens moped just inside the exit to the grounds. Above the door, a holosign flashed the word "closed." Austin noticed and offered to take some holos with them, which perked them right up. I began snapping holos as Austin balanced each kid on a knee and posed. He laughed and joked with them in a natural, easygoing manner. I had fun despite my best attempts not to. So much fun that by the time we walked into the blinding light and breath-stealing cold of the arctic, I'd nearly forgotten what we were there for.

That ended as the drones flew overhead with recording lights on. I held up an arm to shield myself. The sun reflected off the snowy ground around us. It was hard to keep an eye on what was happening until Austin offered me a sunshade, which I gratefully snapped over my eyes.

My heart sunk when I processed the sheer number of drones surrounding the area.

"It's the time of day," Austin said.

"It's not the sun I'm worried about," I whispered back, and he seemed to notice the hovercams for the first time.

His response was to put an arm around me and pull me to his

side. It was unexpected, and I stumbled, but the security of his embrace helped as he marched us through the mele to the small hill ahead.

"How about we take a sled and see if we can outrun them?" Austin offered against my ear. His hot breath, so contrasting to the weather, sent shivers down my body.

I couldn't help but smile and nod. We crested the top of the hill and found a far longer descent on the other side. Bright red sleds sat on top of the hill in rows along with ski equipment and snowboards tucked into compartments of AC glass for easy access.

Austin let go of me and gestured to the nearest sled. I climbed on and felt him settle in behind me. His body pressed against my torso and his long legs wrapped around mine. He reached in front of us to grab hold of the rope and press a button on the sled just as a camera swooped in front of my face.

"A button?" I asked.

In answer, he pushed it, and I was thrown back into him as we whipped forward and down the hill, leaving the camera behind.

The solar-powered sled felt like it had rockets firing out the back end as Austin steered us in a zigzag down the hill at incredible speed, avoiding the hovercams each time they floated toward us. With nothing in the way and the feeling of flying, I reached out my arms to either side, threw my head back, and whooped.

When we glided to the bottom of the hill, Austin whispered, "Hold on," and pushed the button again. We flew forward, snow spraying on either side of us as we glided through the center of two walls made of snowy bricks. He pulled the rope hard, and we tipped sideways as he spun us around the edge of one of the walls. I screamed like a kid on a roller coaster and laughed as we came to a sudden stop.

Behind the wall sat a veritable mountain of pre-prepped snow-balls, waiting for a fight with the equally snowy fort on the opposite side. But I didn't want to be on the opposite side from Austin. I was completely comfortable right there, between his legs, and found myself disappointed it was over.

"They'll find us in a minute," he said, climbing off and removing the extra warmth of his body I'd felt even through his layers of clothing.

I wanted to cry but knew I had to behave like an adult, so I followed suit, standing on wobbly legs.

"What do we do?" I asked since he seemed at home playing in the snow.

"Take aim," he said, handing me a snowball.

Following his lead, I climbed to the top of the snow wall and waited. Sure enough, the hovercams sped into view, pausing just between the walls.

"Now!" Austin shouted and let his weapon fly. It smacked into the drone right over the camera, and the whole thing wobbled tenuously in the air.

I laughed and let loose with a barrage of snowballs along with him until the drones fled and we'd made enough of a dent in the ready-made pile that we could no longer reach them easily from our vantage point.

We both collapsed onto our asses in the snow with our backs against the wall, laughing.

"Not so bad," he said after catching his breath.

I turned toward him to find him leaning into me.

"No," I agreed. "I think we may have ambushed them instead of vice versa."

"You have me on your side," he said, pulling up his ski mask to reveal his face. "I won't let you down."

I bit my lip and flipped up my own mask I'd grabbed in hurried preparation for our playground adventure, allowing the icy air to kiss my face. Considering the warmth coming off Austin, the Arctic cold didn't feel so bad. It was like he had his own furnace burning inside. Then the smile he shot my way eclipsed even that.

"Seriously, Rosi. I'm sorry they keep doing this to you. I know I work for them, but I'm not a bad guy. I'll do everything I can to make things more comfortable for you."

"I appreciate that," I said, leaning in because he also seemed to have his own gravitational pull. To prevent throwing myself at him and regretting it, I added, "I had fun."

He beamed, and a genuine smile made his eyes light up like liquid silver. My insides melted along with them, and my body practically cried to finish the distance between us.

"I did too," he said. "We should go for another ride when there are no cameras around."

I nodded, and he inched forward, only a breath away. The kiss felt inevitable, but I forced myself to wait for him to initiate it. The last thing I needed was to have misread the signs from Austin Cooper and be too mortified to go on the expedition.

My chest rose and fell faster the closer he came. His head tilted, and his lips opened. His breath tasted of mint. But just as we connected, something whooshed over our heads, and I jerked back, staring up at the camera light of a drone in horror.

Austin pulled his ski mask down and stood to swat the drone away, tossing a snowball after it for good measure. The thing sizzled and crashed in the ground.

He stood still, taking slow, deep breaths as I rose and readjusted my own face covering. The moment was ruined, but the look in his eyes said maybe not forever.

I put a hand on his arm, and he looked at me.

"Let's go back inside. Maybe have a cup of cocoa?" I offered.

I could tell he was smiling even beneath the mask, but it didn't reach his eyes, which meant it was the one he reserved for the cameras hovering nearby again despite the demise of their predecessor. "I should take you back, you're right."

I wanted to press him for more but didn't want to do so in front of the cameras. So I followed him back to the sled and tried to enjoy the tame ride back up the hill. When we headed for the building, Austin turned around and waved at the hovercams like it had all been in good fun. And when we got inside, he offered me his hand to shake.

Confused, I stared at it as I pulled off my mask and gloves. Did he regret what almost happened? Because I didn't.

Lowering his hand after leaving it up for far too long, Austin cleared his throat. "I'm glad you had fun, Rosi. I'm sure our excursion will be fun too. I'll be in touch to discuss things next week. Enjoy the rest of your stay."

He spun on his heel and walked away on long legs far too fast to catch up to unless I wanted to appear obviously desperate. My insides were a jumbled mess. Was he leading me on? Did he...do that for the cameras?

Feeling ill, I hurried back to my suite. No, I decided. I'd gotten a glimpse of the real Austin, even if for a moment, and he wasn't faking that. But that didn't mean I wouldn't be getting into more baggage than I bargained for if I pursued this. And I had bigger cryptids to fry while I was here.

Don't lose sight of the goal, Rosi.

7

AUSTIN

W<small>HEN</small> I <small>GOT BACK TO MY ROOM,</small> I <small>ORDERED HOT COCOA WITH EXTRA</small> marshmallows and sipped it as I sat cross-legged, staring out at the scenery. That had been too close for comfort, or maybe too comfortable to be close. I liked Rosi. A lot. And it wasn't just my libido reacting. But starting something with her was out of the question. Not only did I put myself at risk professionally, but I would also put her in danger by getting close. I wasn't ready to do that yet again, maybe not ever. I had to take control of my emotions and recenter, that was all.

But drinking the hot chocolate reminded me of her sweetness and how much I craved that kind of sugar. *It's just as bad for your body as the real kind*, I reminded myself. As I placed the empty cup down on the kitchen counter for the cleaning bots, I felt no guilt though. A treat once in a while was necessary after all.

I sat on the yoga mat, still on the floor since this morning, and began my meditation again, breathing in and out as I watched the light fill me and carry away the dark. Surrendering myself to the emptiness of my mind, I relaxed into a state of complete awareness.

Until Rosi's vanilla scent filled the air, and I opened my eyes, convinced she was there, and thoroughly excited about it. But she wasn't there. I had all but dumped her before anything even started. It was the right choice even if it felt horrible. She deserved someone who could keep her happy and away from a dangerous life like the one I lived. I couldn't be trusted. I didn't want to be responsible for anyone but myself. The possible repercussions made my heart stutter and my throat threaten to close. But that wasn't going to happen. I wouldn't let it.

Then why was I so antsy? I stood to pace and ended up leaving my suite. Maybe I'd do a half-grav run around the track at the top of the resort. The 360-degree views made it my favorite spot so far, and I didn't think many tourists used it, especially in the late afternoon.

I glanced at number 600 as I boarded the upward tube, wondering if she'd be leaving the same time as I was. Luckily, nothing happened. Yet I continued to stare as I made my way to the smaller, interior dome that sat above the center of the top floor of the resort.

No one was up there when I got out, and I smiled, hands on my hips. I could enjoy the view of the vast natural beauty that stretched out below me like a down blanket as I ran, getting into sync with the rhythm of my body. It was another form of meditation for me. I stretched out my hamstrings and did a few lunges to warm up. Then I was off, having set my gravity to fifty percent using my specialized shoes, which made me lighter and worked an entirely different set of muscles than a normal run would. The untouched landscape helped ground me, and I began to relax into a steady pace, feeling in my element, which was away from the complications of man.

I'd just rounded the final bend of my second lap when the tube settled back up and deposited a group of teenage girls onto the track. The minute they spotted me, the giggling started. Like a good paid celebrity, I smiled and waved as they started to snap holovids. This was what I hated about the celebrity status that came with the sports. I wasn't a person. I was an icon, a fantasy no one could possibly live up to. But if it got me to the asteroid belt, it'd be worth it.

The entrance to the tubes remained blocked as four sets of eyes watched me like I was the zebra and they were the pride of lions waiting to tear me to shreds. What was I supposed to do, turn around and run the other way?

Bluffing through them was my best bet, I decided, as I came around the third time.

"Austin!" one girl yelled just as I thought about slowing down and strolling past them with a smile.

Figured. So I nodded in their direction and kept running past. They'd get tired eventually, and I had enough stamina for at least ten more laps before I'd have to cool down. Women always sexualized me, and it sucked. I understood better than most men how women felt when being ogled. It was another thing I'd appreciated about Rosi, come to think of it. Sure, she accidentally announced to the world she was hoping to fuck me, but she insisted it was a mistake instead of testing the waters. It both helped and hurt. It helped because if she wasn't interested, then I had less to worry about. It hurt because it made me that much more interested in her. In fact, if the tubes hadn't malfunctioned, I'd have had to figure out how to hide my hard-on from her. Thankfully, that little accident cooled me off enough to settle down.

Shit, I was coming around again, and this time there were only two of them, the others having run out onto the track, but that was still two too many.

"Austin, can you take us out on a private excursion?" The blond interloper asked, reaching out to latch on to my arm as I passed.

I stopped, leaning over to grab my knees, more to avoid her grip and think through my response than catch my breath. Then I glanced up, smiling what my mom called my million-dollar smile. "Sorry, ladies. Only one winner of the grand prize. But I hope you have fun on your trip."

The blond pouted, and her friend froze like a deer in headlights, mouth hanging open. "There's no rule against hanging out while on vacation though." The blond tossed her hair and tucked her shoulders back so her ample bosom popped further out of her bra. She'd get herself injured if she thought it was a good idea to wear that kind of lingerie for exercise.

"Sorry, ladies. I'm spoken for. Have a good run." I pushed past her and was about to step into the tube when one of them grabbed my ass.

I spun around, backing up into the tube, my face hot as hades. Anger and embarrassment blinded me at the same time as the girls giggled furiously.

Then the tube suddenly went into free fall, and their giggles turned to screams.

8

ROSI

APPARENTLY, WHEN ILA HAD SAID MEET IN THE MORNING SHE'D MEANT before noon, not at four p.m. standard time. I felt terrible when I showed up to the museum and she was in the middle of one of her craft classes with a handful of kids. I wanted to blame my tardiness on the playground and Austin, but the truth was I hadn't even woken up in enough time to make it. She'd chastised me in a friendly way and shooed me off to have fun, promising to talk to me tomorrow if I could manage to get up a couple hours earlier.

I guess I had some sleep to make up for last night, but I doubted that would happen again, especially if I set an alarm. Meanwhile, I had to figure out a way to get Austin to talk to me about the expedition sooner than next week. I needed a plan in place and was sure that our almost kiss earlier complicated things for him enough to want to avoid me. I should've shaken his hand when he offered it, not burned a bridge. It was just so shocking.

The sound of screams stopped me in my tracks. I glanced up at the bottom of the waterfall to find one of the clear tubes whipping around like an amusement park ride, a figure hanging off the edge as it jerked and twisted in every direction.

Was that...Austin? *Shit.* I glanced around, looking for something —anything that might help—and came up short.

"It has to be a publicity stunt," said a man about twenty yards away, crossing his arms over his chest.

But I didn't think so. Not when there wasn't a single hovercam in sight or when Austin lost his grip with one hand. The tube flung him around like a kid trying to shake off a spider. Even he couldn't possibly hold on for long.

The only thing that even hinted at a soft landing was the tank of water at the bottom of the waterfall. But it wasn't more than five feet deep. Even if he could aim that well, there was no way he'd come out of his fall intact.

My heart stuttered as I scanned the area. Someone nearby screamed as the tube hit against the rocks with a crash that threatened to burst my ear drums.

I spotted a kid wearing hover disks, bobbing about three feet above the ground. I dashed forward and grabbed them off his feet, barely listening to his profane response as I turned back to the mayhem to find Austin finally lose his grip and plummet from the top of the resort.

He rotated into a controlled dive toward the waterfall, and I tossed the hover disks as hard as I could, like frisbees toward him.

"Austin catch!" I screamed.

It was like watching an action star on a holovid. In what felt like slow motion, he twisted in midair, catching a disk beneath each foot and spreading his arms like he was on a balance beam as he skidded through the air just above the water, finally hitting the surface and tumbling inside the frothy soup.

I ran for the clear wall and jumped, lifting myself so I could peer over the edge of the AC glass and search for any signs of life.

The hover disks popped up first like unsinkable pool floaters. As I chewed a mouthful of hair, searching the bubbles and freezing spray with waning hope, up came Austin's hand, followed by his golden head.

"Here!" I reached out to him, and in moments he'd grasped my arm with one hand and the side of the wall with the other.

Face inches from mine, his chest heaved as water streamed from him. His pupils had dilated so much that the black almost overtook the gray completely. I tried to find words, any words at all, but couldn't. So silently, I helped him climb over the side as people cheered like it had been some sort of rehearsed show. Water splashed all over me, plastering my clothes to my body, but I didn't care.

By the time we were both on the ground in front of the fountain, I was as soaked and shivering as he was, and the crowd had gathered around to take vids and snapshots of the moment.

"This isn't a show. What is wrong with you people?" I yelled, stepping in front of him, arms spread.

Even the kid who lost his hover disks seemed to be enjoying himself. And since no one moved to help, I raised my wristcom and called for medical help.

Austin stayed weirdly still as I shooed away the crowds. He focused on breathing and kept his eyes closed. But having been soaked so thoroughly, he couldn't hide the trembling in his body. Finally, I too felt the cold I would have expected being near so much snow and ice. But how much was the temperature of the water and how much was trauma, I had no clue for either of us. When the last of the stragglers backed away, I noted a smear of blood across Austin's knuckles and sat beside him, tentatively placing my hand over his. I wiped it gently with my thumb. He opened his eyes and gave me a grateful and almost shy smile. It was only when the hovercot finally arrived and we'd been transported to the medcenter and given blankets and something for the shock that I found my voice, hoarse as it was.

"What the hell happened?" I asked, interrupting his breathing exercises again.

He looked up at me as though he'd just realized I was still there with him. "I don't know. I was in a hurry to leave the track, and it just collapsed as I stepped on it."

I wondered why he'd been in a hurry to leave but thought that might be a strange question considering what happened.

"I can't believe you survived that. If it had been anyone else..." I let my voice trail off.

Austin swallowed and nodded. "You saved my life. That was quick thinking, Rosi."

"I couldn't just stand there and watch you plummet to your death. I'm surprised it worked." The truth of my words shocked me as much as the actual event.

"I mean, it is what I do," Austin said with a weak laugh. "But I usually have time to mentally prepare."

"I was about to look for you when you decided to make your grand entrance," I said, deciding to go along with his humor. It seemed the best option under the circumstances.

Austin rewarded me with one of his genuine grins that made my heart flutter. I knew I'd made the right call.

"So you had an ulterior motive for saving my life?" he asked, his voice hitting that low vibrato that made me squeeze my thighs tighter together.

If you died, I'd never see those gorgeous stormy eyes again. Was what I wanted to say. But instead, I went with, "You owe me an expedition, Mr. Cooper. I'm not letting anything happen to you until I've cashed in."

Austin laughed at that and shook his head.

His eyes met mine, and something inside of me snapped, like a loose wire clicking into place.

The door burst open, and in walked Nicole flanked by a handsome man and Cora, who pushed her way in front of Nicole and sank to her knees in front of me, grabbing my hands.

"Are you okay?"

"I'm fine, chica," I said in a low whisper. "It was Austin who almost died."

"What happened?" Nicole asked. The man behind her grasped her shoulders as though keeping her grounded.

"The tube malfunctioned again," I said. "Only worse this time. It nearly killed Austin and anyone else who would have been unlucky enough to be beneath it." I stood on cold, shaky legs and decided I was angry enough to go with some snark. "I guess there must've been an extra sun flare."

Nicole cut her gaze to me like a knife, but it only lasted a second before she regained control and fell into damage control mode.

"We have a team of engineers on it. In the meantime, we're bringing the backup elevators online. Thank goodness you are both okay."

Austin stood as well, clutching the blanket tucked around his shoulders. "It was Rosi's quick thinking that saved me. If I hadn't had those few seconds on the hover disks, I would've hit too hard and fast."

"Well thank you, Ms. Sanchez," Nicole said. "We are all lucky you won the trip. Now I suggest you both go to your rooms, take a hot shower or bath, and relax. I will have dinner sent up to each of you and throw in a massage at the spa, on the house."

I plastered on a smile and waited for Nicole and her shadow to leave before turning to Austin again. "You should almost die more often. Free room service and massages are totally worth it."

Cora backed up a little with a funny grin on her face. "I hate to mention it, but since you're going out for a massage, I was hoping to have the room tonight."

The banter I'd gotten so good at dried up on my tongue. "What? Why?"

"I met someone. He's part of the band that plays down at the Polar night club. I kind of have a date."

Where the fuck was I supposed to go? I was freezing and dripping wet, and okay, maybe more than a little stressed.

"Why don't you go up to Austin's room?" Cora asked, eyebrows raised in his direction like a dare to defy her.

"Don't be ridiculous," I blurted. "Austin has better things to do than entertain me after a near death experience. Why can't you go to this musician's room?"

"He shares it with his brother, who has dibs tonight. Besides, Austin's used to near death experiences. He thrives on them, don't you, Austin? You don't mind Rosi hanging out, do you?"

"You have two bedrooms," he answered.

"Actually," I said, recalling the last time I had a "girls" weekend with Rosi and she ended up having an orgy in the cabin we rented, "she, um…" I almost choked on the words as I tried to explain the way some of her friends had decided it might be nice to roll into my room and fuck on the floor. Or how when I ran out to the main room to find her, I'd instead been confronted with a group of no less than five people bent in ways that made me assume they were part of the circus. I'd ended up camping in the woods that night, pretty sure if there were any cryptids they'd been scared off by the noises coming from the cabin.

"I tend to like things on the wild side," Cora said in an attempt to save me the explanation. She winked and bit her tongue. "We may need use of the entire premises. There may also be others involved. If you want to join us you're more than wel—"

"It's fine," Austin said, his voice so soft I almost didn't hear him. "You can stay with me. I have two bedrooms and tons of extra clothes. We can order the room service Nicole promised for dinner, and you can go to sleep early. I know I could use a good night's rest after that."

Cora clapped and fled the room before I could get a hold of her. But I'd catch up to her eventually…after spending the night in Austin Cooper's room.

9

AUSTIN

ALREADY THINGS WERE NOT GOING TO PLAN. INSTEAD OF AVOIDING Rosi for the week, I now had her staying in my resort room. Her clothes still heavy with water, clung to every tempting curve and muscle in her body. I found it hard to not stare. She was so much more substantial than the wispy models who were always trying to court me. I appreciated a healthy body, and Rosi's curved in all the right places.

So my first stop was my dresser. I tossed her a white T-shirt and a pair of jogging shorts with a drawstring, figuring pants would be too long. Then I peeled off my own shirt and headed for the shower before stopping short.

"Sorry," I said, turning around. "Ladies first." I gestured to the alcove and the shower that was far nicer than the one in the secondary bedroom. My cock twitched when I realized she was staring at my chest and twisting a molasses-colored curl around her finger.

"Oh." She tore her eyes from my pectorals, and the skin around her face and neck darkened. "No. You go ahead. I'll be fine. I'll just change here real quick."

I'd never wanted to invite someone into the shower with me

more than I did in that moment. But I knew it wasn't a good idea. When the lights blinked, I shook my head and strode into the bathroom, already starting my deep breathing.

But even as I ducked under the steaming waterfall, all I could picture was Rosi peeling off her wet clothes and climbing into the shower. So I grabbed my shaft and started stroking it, eager to put an end to any more thought vacations before I did something I'd regret.

Besides, she wouldn't even shake my hand earlier. She clearly had second thoughts about our almost kiss.

When I came out of the shower in fresh sweatpants, Rosi was sitting on the living room sofa, her knees tucked under her chin. My gaze traveled down the long path of her thighs to where the curve of her ass hid just inside the dark material of my shorts.

"Thanks," I said, getting her attention.

She let her legs down and stood. I would have been disappointed except that the white T-shirt revealed the nubs of her nipples beneath the material. No bra. Of course there was no bra. I didn't have an extra one for her.

My cock twitched again. *Traitor.*

"I...um, ordered room service. I didn't know what you like so I got a whole bunch of stuff. I figured it's on Nicole, so..."

"Great," I said, swinging my arms like an awkward teenager. "I'm not picky. Though I could use some protein."

"Good. I ordered the seafood platter. I also got a basket of onion rings. Comfort food."

I smiled, relaxing a little. "I love onion rings. Haven't had them in years."

"Unhealthy?" she asked, tilting her head so a curl flopped in her face.

"Not easy to find in Tibet or the Sahara." I grinned. I couldn't help trying to impress her. The sound of her laugh gave me the same adrenaline rush as scaling a mountain with my bare hands.

"Well, you're in luck then because I ordered something else just for fun."

"Oh?" I asked, moving into the room and flopping down on the couch so she'd sit next to me.

"S'mores. They bring us some sticks and the fixings and we roast them over a tiny campfire." She rocked back onto the seat beside me and stuck her hands behind her head, proud of herself.

Of course that also had the effect of showing off her prominent nipples again.

I cleared my throat. "So you said you wanted to find me earlier? Before I fell from the sky?"

Rosi sat up straight and picked at the edge of the T-shirt that was far too long on her.

"Yes. We didn't have much of a chance to talk while avoiding the cameras earlier and when you called this morning, I got the feeling something was...off."

Smart, resourceful, and perceptive. This woman was a triple threat. "I was just stressed."

She hummed, and I got the impression she didn't buy it. Luckily, we were saved by the arrival of dinner.

We set up on the floor in front of the fireplace on the thick white rug that was supposed to be imitation polar bear.

"So you study mythology?" I asked. Keeping her talking about herself was a good way to prevent her from questioning me about Nicole's fabrication. Besides, I was interested.

She straightened and rocked a little like she was embarrassed. "Yeah. I study various cultures and their mythos. I'm interested in the Inuit and hoping to add to my dissertation material while I'm here." She took a big bite of onion ring, and I longed to smear the oil from her plump lips to other parts of her body.

"That's amazing," I said. "One of my favorite parts of traveling is interacting with different people and learning from them."

Rosi stopped eating, letting her onion ring drop to the plate. She scooted closer. "Really?"

"That and the wildlife. I love seeing animals in their natural habitat."

Rosi seemed thoughtful for a moment. I could tell there was something she was holding back. I wanted to pry it out of her, but according to everything I'd learned about her, the best way to do that was to be patient and let her organize her thoughts.

"I am studying something like that," she finally said. "A combination of those things really." She popped a shrimp in her mouth and leaned back on her hands, surveying me.

Assuming she was checking to see if I was truly interested, I leaned toward her. I was definitely interested. "So what's your research about?"

"I'm studying cryptids." It came out fast and explosive, like she either forced it out, or it escaped her lips.

"What's a cryptid?" I asked, not breaking eye contact. Her dark chocolate eyes sparkled with unmistakable excitement, and heat swelled in my belly. I loved being the source of that excitement.

"It's a creature that people can't explain the existence of, so most of the time they assume it's not real."

"I see." I thought for a moment. "I've seen things in my travels—not creatures per say, but things most people wouldn't believe. Personally, I think dismissing something because it makes you uncomfortable is shallow thinking. There's a lot more to this world than we currently understand."

"Exactly!" Rosi dove toward me, and for a moment I thought she was going to hug me, but she ended up sitting with her face cradled in hands, scooted so close that the only thing between us was a mostly eaten plate of onion rings. "It's so good to find someone who gets it. Sometimes the myths of a culture come from reality. It's those stories I'm interested in. I want to prove to the world that these things are out there whether they like it or not. I want proof that no one can look away from even when it makes them uncomfortable."

I swallowed. I wanted to tell her the chances of finding something like that on our hellipod journey was as close to zero as it got. I also wanted to kiss her candy-apple lips. But I needed to abstain from both, so I inhaled deeply and counted to three before answering.

She leaned back, shoulders slumping as she examined the onion rings left on the plate. "You think that's crazy."

"No!" She'd mistaken the reason for my discomfort. I grabbed her hand so she'd look at me. "I think it's noble to want to wake up the world."

Staring into my eyes, her mouth parted invitingly. My fingers circled the soft skin of her hand, and she sighed in response. My cock betrayed me once again, but I decided not to fight it that time, to just be in the moment. This kind of contact was still appropriate, at least that's what I decided to tell myself.

But when she leaned in and tilted her head, I recalled what I had almost done in the snow and knew I had to stop it.

"That's why you always wear those funny shirts, right? I've seen you in a couple now. The bigfoot one and the one that...got wet." Damn it, that wasn't helping.

But she did break out of the trance she'd seemed to be in and straightened up, reclaiming her hand. "You noticed those?"

"Hard not to," I said and cleared my throat. I hoped that didn't come across wrong. I meant it as a compliment on the humor not an *I've been staring at your breasts for two days* sort of comment.

Thankfully, she took it the right way and smiled. "You notice details, don't you?"

"I have to. Sometimes the smallest thing will make the difference between life and death."

"Like a boy using hover disks nearby?" She rewarded me with a smile.

"Like a boy using hover disks."

Torn between kissing her and telling her everything I'd never shared with anyone, I chose neither option. Instead, I stood and cleared the dishes, placing them on the ample counter rimmed in what appeared to be deadly looking icicles for the cleaning bots to deal with in the morning.

When I turned around again, Rosi had set up a tiny barbecue on the carpet and was sticking marshmallows onto tiny metal spears.

"Dessert?" I asked, impressed with her appetite.

"You have to try at least one." She handed me one of the spears as I scooted onto the floor beside her. I watched her face in the glow of the small fire, my gaze traveling down the curve of her neck to her breasts.

Clearing my throat, I reached over her to snatch a graham cracker and pre-cut piece of chocolate. Her eyes sparkled in the light as she sucked in her lower lip when she found me an inch away. Slowly, I sat back in my spot to prevent myself from copying her and sucking in her lower lip as well.

We assembled our sandwiches in silence, the air thick with tension. Then she took an enormous bite of her s'more and moaned in ecstasy. My cock was so hard I had to shift as she reached forward to offer me a bite, one hand held below the melting contents of the treat.

She swallowed as I took an equally huge bite, her chest heaving like she was having trouble controlling her breathing. The decadent flavors slid down my throat, and she stuffed the remainder in her mouth, chewing quickly, eyes wide.

A dollop of chocolate gathered at the corner of her mouth, and I reached forward to wipe it away, letting the pads of my fingers slip lazily over her skin. Her long lashes swept the tops of her cheeks as she closed her eyes.

It would have been so easy to taste her then, to lay her down on the soft rug and explore each of her curves and valleys that I'd been obsessed over since she stepped foot off the jet. But the vulnerability of the moment stole my breath, and the aching fear of hurting someone I might care about stopped me from acting on my impulses.

Tenderly, I brushed the last of the chocolate from her skin and pulled away, standing and stretching as I faced away from her, waiting for my erection to subside. Rosi couldn't understand the danger I posed, but I wasn't being entirely selfless either. Every split-second, life and death decision I made in the heat of the moment was a gamble. One wrong step and my life was forfeit on any of my adventures. It was a reality I had made peace with long ago. But someone else's life depending on my decisions? That was not so easy to disregard. I knew from experience. I knew because of the constant battle to still my mind when the vision of Sara's angry face threatened to invade my consciousness.

Turning around at the sobering thoughts swimming in my mind, I found Rosi on her feet, mid-yawn. "It's getting pretty late, and we're both tired," I lied.

She nodded, covering her mouth in an adorably embarrassed way after being caught.

"Go ahead and get some sleep then." I nodded toward the spare bedroom.

"Thanks, Austin. Sorry about my roommate. I didn't intend to impose on you like this."

"I've enjoyed the company," I said truthfully. "It's been awhile since I've hung out with a friend."

Rosi startled, and I wondered if it was because of the friend word. Had she been feeling the same pull I had? I didn't think I'd imagined the way she'd leaned into my touch, but danger lights flashed in my head...

"Yeah. Well, it's nice to connect with someone who doesn't think I'm bat-shit crazy."

I laughed. "I'm sure not that many people do."

Her smile melted off her face as she looked down and away. "Actually, Cora's the only one who doesn't. Even my parents never believed me. Um, I mean my dissertation advisor was supportive of my research after some convincing."

Furrowing my brow, I stepped close enough to lift her chin so she'd face me. "Your parents didn't believe what exactly?"

She shifted uncomfortably but didn't pull away from my hold.

"I saw one when I was ten. A cryptid. I'm ninety percent sure it was a sasquatch." The skin of her face warmed beneath my touch, but she met my eyes once again, daring me to challenge her.

"That must have been incredible," I whispered.

She relaxed, and I reluctantly let go, but we stayed so close I could smell her vanilla scent.

I avoided sugar in my diet when possible, but sometimes I gave in to the cravings like I had earlier with the s'mores. I was tempted to give in again to her sweet scent.

"It was amazing. It was like time stopped. We were on a camping trip in the redwoods at the northern tip of California. I'd always loved the enormity of the giant trees and liked to imagine that they'd been born before people had. I guess I was a bit of a dreamer even then, but there was something magical and other-worldly about the air there, like a hush that protected against the rest of the world. I wandered away from our campsite that day, chasing a butterfly that I pretended was a fairy, and that's when I saw it."

Her eyes filled with a light that pulled at me. When she drew in a breath, I found myself leaning in toward her.

"I remember craning my head back to see the top of him just like I would one of the trees. He was covered in matted, brown fur and had these big, brown, human-like eyes."

"That must've been scary for you." I pictured a ten-year-old Rosi running into a giant animal and longed to pull her into my chest, but she laughed in response to my assertion.

"No actually, that was the weird part. I wasn't scared at all. I was fascinated. And his eyes were so expressive. He was just as surprised to see me."

"What happened?" I asked, completely entranced.

"He backed away slowly and kind of...melted into the forest. I mean, yes, he was the same color as the massive trunks, but it was more like he disappeared right before my eyes. I stood there for what felt like forever but was probably only several minutes trying to wrap my brain around the experience, then ran back to camp to tell my parents." Her face fell, and the pain there made it nearly impossible not to reach for her. "They scolded me for making up stories and leaving their sight. Not that they'd been looking or even missed me."

"I'm sorry," I said, hurting for her. I couldn't imagine my mother doing anything but encouraging everyone around her.

Waving a hand, she shrugged. "Don't be. They are who they are. I just wonder sometimes, what would it have been like if they'd listened?" She frowned and averted her gaze again.

"So you've been searching for proof ever since?" I asked to regain her attention. I hated seeing her sadness and wanted to recapture the magic in her expression when she'd shared her story with me.

It worked. She met my eyes again and I saw an eager gleam.

"I will find proof of cryptid existence and share it with the world. They are a scientific reality." She actually stomped her foot, and I'd never realized until that moment how much stubbornness turned me on.

Fuck it. I pulled her in before I could think or breathe, and the next thing I inhaled was her mouth, lips just as plump and sweet as I'd imagined.

Rosi stiffened for a second, and I leaned away, afraid I'd misread her. Then she shoved me backward onto the couch and straddled me.

We looked at each other as her chest rising and falling rapidly. I should have stopped it, but she leaned down and met my lips again, swiping her tongue across the seam until I opened to her and met her tongue in a dance of exploration.

I pressed her body to me, running my palms up her back beneath my own T-shirt. She gasped at the skin-to-skin contact, and I took the opportunity to taste the sensitive pulse point on her throat. She moaned as I teased the area with my teeth before licking then sucking in the caramel skin I'd been dying to try.

Groaning, she mashed her core against my growing erection, sliding her heat across it until I too moaned my appreciation.

The lights blinked then exploded in a shower of sparks around us. The arm of the sofa suddenly burst into flames. I shifted her to my other side away from the fire. I reached for my shirt to smother it, only to realize I wasn't wearing one.

But Rosi stuffed hers in my hand, and I had things under control in a matter of moments. Once I was sure it was out, I turned and found her arms crossed over her nipples, the tops of her breasts pressed up in small mounds. While the fire had made me soften, my cock returned to a semi-erect state as I stared at her, half-bared before me.

"What the fuck is happening?" she asked, distracting me again.

Right. Breathe.

I closed my eyes and did the mental exercise I was so accustomed to.

"Be right back," I said as the soft blue glow below the glass icicle counters lit my path to the bedroom. I returned moments later with another shirt for her.

She looked up from where she'd been examining the burn on the sofa and snatched the shirt from the air. She quickly turned to put it on, but not before I got a peek at her perfect breasts with pert nipples that made me want to suck on them like Luxardo cherries.

Breathing in again, I closed my eyes. When I opened them, she was facing me, arms crossed over her chest, this time in a hunter-green shirt.

"You're avoiding the question," she pointed out.

Sighing, I collapsed back onto the sofa and ran a palm over my face. "Yeah, because I don't know what's happening. But I also don't buy Nicole's excuse. Solar flares? I mean, I doubt they'd have opened the resort if it was that sensitive. They're still trying to put the whole Paradise Atlantis business out of the public memory."

Rosi sat beside me and placed a hand on my knee. "So she asked you to lie to me?"

"I think she's lying to both of us. I think she's fucking scared of something and is trying to cover it up so she doesn't start a panic."

Rosi sank into the cushions. "That's ominous."

"Yeah."

We stared at the ceiling for a moment when the door buzzed.

"Come in," I said, sitting up straight.

The door slid open to reveal the man I'd seen with Nicole on more than one occasion. I noticed several people in the hall behind him as he slipped inside, but the door shut before I could make out who they were.

"Hi," he said, glancing over at Rosi on the sofa. "I'm Jackson Meadows. I'm an engineering consultant for Bennet Systems. We had reports of multiple fires on this floor. Is everything okay?"

"We were able to put it out before it did any more damage," I said, indicating the burn spot on the sofa next to me. "Do you know what caused it?"

"That's what we're investigating," Jackson answered. "Nicole was concerned and asked me to check on you both. Luckily, it seems I can do so at the same time."

Rosi cleared her throat and glanced to the side.

"There's something going on in this resort, and it's potentially dangerous," I said, ignoring his comment.

"It's not the sun. So don't go there," Rosi added as he opened his mouth to reply.

"We don't know what happened. That was a theory, but now it seems less likely," Jackson said.

"Wait. Did you say this happened to the whole floor?" Rosi jumped to her feet.

"Yes, it appears so," Jackson said.

"Cora!" Rosi rushed past Jackson and out into the hall.

I groaned as one of the only lights that hadn't exploded did so above us.

Jackson eyed it thoughtfully.

"You need to tell people whatever is going on here," I said, standing. I spread my hands in what I hoped was a peaceful yet reasonable gesture. "If there's a design issue, it's better to call things off now than wait until something worse happens."

Jackson eyed me with the same expression he had the lightbulb. "So you're a PR specialist now, Mr. Cooper?"

"No, but I care about people's lives and so should you," I snapped. My wristband sparked and I yanked it off, tossing it to the side incredulously. "This is getting ridiculous."

"So far every malfunction has one thing in common," Jackson said, getting my attention back.

"Electricity?" I asked, grateful he was focusing on addressing the situation instead of covering it up.

"No." He backed up a couple of steps, and I noticed his hands fist at his sides. "You."

10

ROSI

I found Cora in the hallway, pacing in front of our room. When she spotted me, we rushed into each other's arms for a hug.

"Thank gods you're okay," she said, releasing me.

"What happened?" I asked, nodding toward the room.

"I don't know. One minute I was reading Jeremy's palm, the next everything exploded."

It was then I noticed the man leaning against the wall covered in ripped leather with muscled arms and tatted sleeves that sported various instruments and musical stanzas. His smooth head glowed under the dim lights of the hallway that I now realized were for emergencies.

I nodded in acknowledgement, and he responded with a salute.

"What about you?" Cora asked, squeezing my arms.

Thinking back to what I'd been doing when it happened, I realized I couldn't tell her. If I did, I'd never hear the end of it. Besides, I wasn't sure it was something that would happen again. Austin and I had probably just got caught up in the moment.

"Same. Well, not the palm reading, but we were on the couch. Talking. And then the lights burst. Austin put out a fire on the furniture. He's good at acting fast under pressure at least."

Cora nodded. "I bet he's good at a lot of things."

I snapped my mouth closed, unwilling to dignify that with a response. But he was good at other things. I could already tell and wanted desperately to continue what we'd started but wasn't sure he'd be into me for more than a minute. It was a stupid idea. There was no way for our relationship to be anything but a whirlwind fuckfest. He was a celebrity and travelled constantly. It was just that when I realized he believed my story without question... Well, he'd gone from sexy as hell to irresistible in a heartbeat.

"Where is he anyway?" Cora asked, stretching to look over my shoulders.

"Jackson Meadows showed up. They're probably still in the room talking. When I realized it wasn't just us that it happened to, I rushed out here to find you."

"You're such a sweetheart." Cora pinched my cheek, and I rolled my eyes in response. "Who's Jackson Meadows?"

"He's Nicole's boytoy." I read up on the history of all the resorts in my research and prep for the trip. When I saw him behind Nicole, that just confirmed the rumors for me. "He's also an engineer."

"Let's go back in there," Cora said, steering me toward Austin's suite. "Maybe we can get some more info on what's happening. Coming, Jeremy?"

"Nah, I'll head back down and see what Sherri's up to. Maybe we can have a threesome later, bae?"

Cora winked. "Sounds nice."

"Wait, you literally only had one person in there? Why'd I have to vacate then?" I whispered as she buzzed Austin's door.

"I just started small. Don't worry, it's vacation and I plan to have fun."

She'd set me up, but I'd enjoyed spending time with Austin, so I let it go. But I wondered if there was an empty suite I could move to so I didn't find myself homeless for the rest of the month or have to impose on Austin for that length of time.

Speaking of, what was taking so long for Austin to answer? A spike of concern shot through me, and I pounded on the doors, stopping short of thumping Jackson on the chest when they slid open.

"Excuse me," he said, slipping by.

Crossing the threshold, I spotted Austin looking miserable on the couch.

"Are you okay?" I asked. "What happened?"

Cora frowned and squinted at a spot just over Austin's shoulder. "Your aura is a mess."

"Thanks?" Austin said before meeting my eyes. "Jackson thinks I had something to do with the electrical issues."

"Shit," I said, kneeling beside him and putting a hand on his leg in what I hoped was a comforting way. "Why?"

"Proximity to all the disasters. Can we talk in private?" he asked, eyeing Cora.

"I know when I'm not wanted. But don't forget if you decide to let loose that we'll be next door and happy for you to join in." She winked at me and wiggled her eyebrows before exiting the room.

Austin's confused expression was welcome as I wasn't about to explain what that meant.

"What's up?" I asked instead, anxious to stay on topic.

"Apparently, what the public doesn't know is that there was sabotage on previous resort grand openings."

I sat back on my heels and thought about my research. "I knew about Paradise Atlantis. Everyone does. But I thought the Time Capsule Resort voyage went well."

"I guess they were able to cover it up," he responded in a hushed voice. "He warned me against telling anyone this and said it would lend evidence toward my guilt."

Ignoring the tiny voice in my head that suggested it might be smart to be suspicious if Jackson thought Austin was likely a saboteur, I squeezed his muscular leg through the thin material of his sweatpants. "I can keep a secret."

He smiled, brushing the hair away from my face. "Thanks. I needed to talk to someone or I'd go crazy."

"I know the feeling," I admitted, rising to sit beside him again. "FYI, it's pretty lame to assume because you were around during the incidents, you're somehow guilty by association."

"Thanks, Rosi. I appreciate that. I have no clue what's happening."

"It seems far more likely that whoever is behind it, assuming it is someone doing it on purpose, is centering their attacks around you because you're the face of the resort."

"Great."

I smiled. "I bet Jackson Meadows doesn't believe in bigfoot."

"Small minds," he agreed and turned his head to face me.

We laughed and stayed there awkwardly staring at each other.

"I...better get some sleep," I said. "And so should you." Though if he followed me into my room, I wouldn't stop him. *Follow me, Austin.*

"You're right. Good night, Rosi." He stood and stopped himself before leaning in for a kiss.

"Yeah. Goodnight." I turned so he wouldn't detect my flush and speed walked to my bedroom.

The moment the doors closed behind me, I released a huge breath and collapsed onto the bed.

If he was some sort of saboteur, would I be safe on the expedition? Why even spend time with me? And why put himself in danger the way he had when he'd fallen off the tube? If I hadn't been there to throw him those hover disks, he'd likely have died, or at least been seriously injured. And I certainly didn't know that would happen.

No, he wasn't doing this. He'd been as preoccupied as me when the lights exploded. His body had definitely responded. There was no faking that.

Crap, now I was hot and bothered again, thinking about his

ample length sliding against me through the friction of our clothing.

I was sweating. I flung off the T-shirt and shorts he'd given me but pulled the tee under the sheet with me so I could inhale his scent. My hand found the spot between my legs craving attention. There was nothing for it but to get through it as soon as I could, so I stroked myself, imagining his nimble fingers instead of my own and how they'd circle the sensitive nub like they had the skin of my back earlier.

Using the pillow, I muffled my moans as I continued picturing him doing all the things to me that I wanted. In my head, his stubble rubbed against the sensitive skin of my thighs, and his tongue explored my folds like it had my mouth.

"Oh god, Austin," I called into my pillow as I came. But instead of being completely satisfied, I only wanted the real thing.

I was falling hard, and that was bad news because even if I complicated things by pursuing the kind of release I wanted, it was something that couldn't continue past this vacation. I had my doctorate to finish, and he... Well, he had adventures to go on that likely didn't involve an extra person tagging along.

Flopping around to my other side, I curled up in a ball and fell into a restless sleep.

I'm ten, and instead of the curious sasquatch, I stare up into the face of my nightmares. Just as tall as the bigfoot I had seen, but far skinnier, it has the head of the tupilaq in the museum with a giant mouthful of needlelike teeth dripping saliva that sizzles as it falls to the earth at my feet. I step backward but am blocked by the trunk of the massive redwood. My knees weaken as my body begins to tremble. The scent of rotting meat overwhelms my senses. Instead of fur, it's covered in gray pock-marked skin that hugs its body like a sleeve for twisted muscle and sinew. Its knees bend backward like a canine, but there are only two. The thing is anything but human, and the terror—the helplessness I feel—blurs my vision and brings tears to my eyes.

Screaming, I wake only to find myself standing naked in the frozen tundra, Austin's blood-soaked body lying prone in front of me. The thing that I faced moments ago bends over him, torn skin and worse stuck between its teeth as it glares at me with human-like, yellow eyes. I back up a few paces, the frozen ground burning against the bottom of my feet. The horror that threatens to suffocate me is no longer from the monster itself but from the vision of Austin's mutilated and lifeless body.

It lunges at me, and I wake again, this time naked in Austin's living room. He stands before me, face filled with concern, muscled chest heaving like he's frightened as well.

I throw myself into his arms, crying, and he holds me close without saying a word. When I finally get myself under control, I pull back and gaze up at him. He smiles, revealing a mouth full of rows of needlelike teeth.

11

ROSI

"Fuck!" I yelled, waking up yet again, completely disoriented as I clutched the sheets to my chest.

Moments later the doors slid open to reveal the same concerned-looking Austin I'd just seen in my dream.

"Stop." I held out a hand and he obeyed. "Open your mouth," I said, tears still streaming down my face.

He furrowed his brow but did as I asked, revealing a set of perfect, white teeth.

I relaxed, leaning back against the headboard. "Okay. Okay this is real."

"This is real," he said carefully, edging around the bed so he could sit at my feet. He rested his hand on my ankle, reminding me that only the thin sheet stood between his hand and my naked body. But the horror and confusion of the nightmare I'd just had stopped my thoughts there.

"You okay? I heard you scream. Nightmare?"

"Yeah." I looked down at the sheet covering me. I didn't want to tell him it was about him. But he probably figured something like that since I made him open his mouth.

"I'm making coffee. Want some?" he offered instead of pressing me.

"That would be amazing," I said, forcing a smile even as I still trembled with the memory of his skin in that thing's mouth. I'd told him yesterday I wasn't afraid of the sasquatch when I was ten.

This was different.

What if that thing really was out there somewhere? What if that's what I found when I went looking? I shuddered. Three times in as many days I'd dreamed of it. But not really, I reminded myself. Austin hadn't appeared until after I met him. And the beast hadn't taken such clear shape until I saw that creepy statue in the museum.

The museum.

"I need to get to my room and get some clothes. I have an appointment in an hour. Can I take a raincheck on coffee?" I asked.

"Sure," Austin said, but the smile he gave me was that same fake one he used for publicity photos, not the real one I'd coaxed out previously.

"Thanks for understanding." I leaned forward, clutching the sheet, and dotted a kiss on his cheek. My own cheeks heated when his stubble rubbed against me, and I recalled in vivid clarity my imagination the previous night.

"I thought it through last night and came up with a sound, logical argument that proves you couldn't have sabotaged anything," I said to change the subject even as I climbed from the bed, securing the sheet around me.

"That's awesome! Thank you. Will you share it with Nicole and Jackson so they don't arrest me ?" His tone was joking, but I detected actual fear beneath the words.

"Of course." Recalling Ila's assertion that she was busy after noon, I added, "Let's meet with them this afternoon. I'll explain then."

"It's a date," Austin said, standing as well. Then the pale skin of his face and neck burned a deep shade of pink. "I mean it's settled."

I nodded and scurried out of the room, making a mad dash for my own door before anyone could see me wearing a sheet. The doors swished open and closed behind me, and I breathed a sigh of relief.

"Good morning," said Jeremy from the kitchen. He was as shirt-less as Austin but far thinner with pierced nipples and a guitar tattooed across his pecs.

"Uh," I said, backing toward my room when Cora and another woman came out of her bedroom. Cora wore a red, lace bra and matching panties, her navel ring on display. The other woman was completely nude, and the second it registered, I averted my gaze. Memories of the cabin incident assaulted me.

"Looks like someone had a good night," Cora said.

I resisted the temptation to look at her. "Yeah. Happy for you. I've got a meeting, so I'm going to grab some clothes and freshen up, then I'll be out of your hair."

I made it to the threshold of my room when Jeremy grabbed my hand and stopped me, his eyes heavy-lidded. "You don't have to rush out, *cher*. You seem wound up. I can help you with that."

"Thanks but no thanks," I said, snatching my hand back. I would not participate in an orgy, especially not one that included my best friend. "I really do have a meeting to get to."

"Suit yourself, love. But the offer stands if you decide to change your mind. Now, where were we, ladies?" He turned back to Cora and the other woman, presumably Sherri, though who knew?

If I hadn't needed a shower so badly, I'd have rushed out in five minutes, but thankfully the water drowned the sound of whatever they were doing, and I was able to relax for the first time in a while as I prepared to meet with Ila and pick her brain.

When I arrived, she was alone and welcomed me into the tiny space she called her office. Pleasant music played in the back-ground as I took the only seat on the opposite side of her desk, which was cluttered with pieces of paper, half-carved dolls, and pictures.

"So you want to know about mythology?" she asked, leaning forward, using her elbows as support. Her hair was braided today, and the lines of her tattoos gave her an air of some sort of ancient knowledge.

"Yes," I said, setting down a cup of coffee for each of us. I'd grabbed them on my way over, knowing I definitely needed some. Opening my notebook, I readied my pen. "Mostly, but I have a lot of questions. I hope you don't mind."

Ila smiled. "I'm an open book, Rosi."

"Let's start with the shaman you mentioned yesterday. The one your husband talks to."

"Ah, the *angakukk*. He's old. I don't know if he really communicates with spirits like he claims he does. I think it's the mushrooms he discovered."

"Is that what *angakukk* usually use to go into a trance?" I asked, leaning in.

She laughed and took a sip of the coffee I'd brought along as a good will offering. I figured I might as well if I was going to get myself some. "No. He's special."

I nodded. "Do you believe in the myths of your people?"

Ila sighed and twisted the cup in her hands. "I think some are stories passed down to teach us lessons, like not wandering off when we're kids."

My encounter in the woods as a child surfaced in my head, but I stayed silent.

"Some were based on fact, but likely embellished over time. The truth is most of my family take the stories for granted, assuming they're as real as seals and polar bears. My mother wholeheartedly believes in Sedna, the queen of the ocean and underworld, for example. She's like a deity who gets pissed when her hair isn't combed."

I smiled. "She can't comb it herself?"

Ila squinted with mischief. "Her father cut off her fingers to get her to stop hanging onto the boat in the legend. He figured their attackers were after her and would leave him alone. Asshole."

We both took a sip of coffee.

"The shaman has to go comb her hair out so she'll bless us with animals to hunt in the water. Or so they say."

I'd read about the myth in my research, but it was interesting to hear her take on it. "What about some of the creatures people say they've spotted out in the wild?" I asked, leaning forward.

Ila shrugged. "Hard to know. Do I think there are *qallupilluk* out there pulling kids beneath the water? I hope not."

"You seem to dismiss the *angakukk* in your village, but do you think there is something to them in general?"

For the first time since we'd started our interview, Ila stiffened, averting her eyes.

"You've seen something?" I pressed.

Ila sighed and sat back in her chair. "My uncle was an *angakukk*. It runs in my mother's family. I never saw anything I couldn't reconcile, but there were moments when he seemed to truly change. And according to my mother, who is otherwise a pretty down-to-earth woman, my grandfather often talked with spirits and even chased shapeshifters away from the outlying families of the village she came from."

"You seem conflicted about that," I said, hoping she'd open up further.

She met my stare. "I don't want you writing something that will have people stereotyping my people as backwards or silly."

"Never. But honestly, I don't think any of what you said is backwards or silly. I think it's amazing." I reached out and patted her hand.

"Thank you. It's not the biggest part of our lives anyway, even if it's a great story. I saw you looking at my tattoos the other day. They're called *kakiniit* and are traditionally exclusive to women. We get them to mark important moments in our lives. These are for the first time I got my period." She gestured to her chin. "I have more on my arms and thighs. They were forbidden for a while because of white settlers."

"I'm so sorry," I said, meaning it.

She nodded. "I know. It was an ugly part of history, but it's important not to forget those sorts of things."

"That's why I'm glad you decided to talk to me," I said twirling my pen between my fingers. "I want to help set the record straight." I stood to leave, realizing it was nearly noon already. But as I closed my notebook, I recalled the creepy statue in the glass case outside the office. "Ila?"

"Yes?" She tossed her empty cup into the recycle bin beside her desk.

"I wanted to know about a specific exhibit out there. The *tupilaq*?" I followed suit with my cup, and a bot zoomed over to empty the receptacle.

"Creepy, isn't it?" she asked, standing. "That one was passed down in my family. I think my great-grandfather made it to chase after someone they'd tossed from the village."

I'd read up on *tupilaq* and cringed inwardly at the idea of her grandfather masturbating over the doll to bring it to life. I didn't even want to ask what it was made of for fear of there being human parts in it.

"It must've been a pretty awful person that got thrown out," I said instead.

She nodded. "Sounds from the stories like he was a pedophile and maybe a murderer. Those kinds of people were tossed out to live on their own, which was all but a death sentence anyway."

I paused at the door when she opened it. "But if that was case, why send a vengeful spirit after him?"

Ila pursed her lips like she wanted this conversation over. "I guess in this case kids were still disappearing from the village."

"Did it work? Did the disappearances stop?" I asked, unable to help myself.

"Yeah. In our village. But whether that was the work of the

elements, the *tupilaq*, or the predator moving elsewhere is anyone's guess. Thanks for stopping by today, Rosi, and thanks for the coffee. That was a real treat. I don't usually drink anything but tea and water."

Her smile was genuine, but her dismissal was unavoidable. I'd gotten a lot of info though and had quite a bit to think about.

On my way out, I paused in front of the offending statue and shivered as the visceral memories of my nightmare flashed in my mind. It made no sense because this creature was made to take out a murdering pedophile. I certainly wasn't that, so it wouldn't be after me, which made the whole thing only a dream, logically. But for some reason my pulse sped up, and I hurried away. In my head I could swear I heard the mocking laugh of a man's baritone voice chase me down the hall.

12

AUSTIN

Rosi caught up with me outside my room. I was about to go find a new wristband when I nearly ran right into her. She darted her gaze around the hall, distracted.

"Did your meeting go okay?" I asked, leading the way around the bend to the largest suite in the resort, the one I knew Nicole would be in.

"Yeah, Ila had lots of great information for me about the Inuit culture. Fascinating stuff."

I nodded in appreciation but couldn't help focusing on this meeting she swore would save my ass. If even a rumor surfaced about me causing this situation, I'd never make it to that asteroid field.

"Where are we?" Rosi asked, seeming to just now notice I'd led her to another room.

"The honeymoon suite." I rapped on the door, deciding the buzzer wasn't trustworthy, being electronic and all.

The door slid open moments later, and I found myself face-to-face with Jackson again. His eyes slid from me over to Rosi then back.

"We're here to talk to Nicole," I said.

"Jackson? Let them in," Nicole called from inside. Her guard dog stepped aside, and I entered, Rosi just behind me.

Nicole sat at the high dining table, long legs crossed at the knee and holopads spread out around her. Even so, she was dressed to the hilt without a hair out of place. She barely glanced up from whatever had her attention but took a sip of a high-price brand of hydropod.

"I don't recall an appointment," she said when she set her drink back down on a hovering coaster.

"I wanted to come," Rosi explained, pushing past me and sitting at the table across from Nicole.

She wore jeans and hiking boots along with a T-shirt that read *The Man The Moth The Legend* with Point Pleasant stamped below that. Rosi and Nicole contrasted like oil and water. But in my mind there was no contest as to who was sexier. I longed to be back on the couch with Rosi before the lights exploded.

"What can I do for you, Ms. Sanchez? I hope your vacation is proving enjoyable." Nicole slid her gaze toward me in a way that insinuated more.

"Until I found out Dr. Meadows accused Austin of sabotage."

Nicole's eyebrows shot up, and Jackson glared daggers at me. He'd told me in no uncertain terms not to share that information with anyone or risk insinuating my own guilt. Shit, I'd brought her here. I really hoped her idea would work.

Breathe.

"Here's the thing," Rosi continued. "If he was responsible, why would he risk his own life yesterday? If I hadn't been there, he'd have died. And last night, we were preoccupied and deep in... conversation when the lights blew. He couldn't have done anything to trigger it."

Nicole tapped her long white nails against the top of the table as she considered Rosi, who fidgeted in response.

"Your sponsorship is important to me," I said, feeling pathetic for groveling.

Rosi tilted her head in question but didn't ask. I appreciated that.

"That makes sense," Nicole said, nodding toward me. "Unless someone outbid our sponsorship." She turned toward Rosi. "And unless you were an accomplice who somehow fixed the contest."

Rosi's face drained of color, much like Nicole's had when I told her about the first incident.

"Rosi had nothing to do with this. Your conspiracy theories are wild accusations," I said, anger swelling in my stomach before I could quell it with calming thoughts or breaths.

Nicole's hovering coaster crashed to the table, spilling water all over her holopads, which sparked and fizzled in response. She stared at the mess, open-mouthed, then leaped from her chair and stalked toward us with eyes like the wicked icicles that surrounded all the countertops.

"That remains to be seen, Mr. Cooper. Believe that I have every resource on this, and that those are extensive, considering who I am. Whoever is responsible for this will pay the price. I promise you that."

"Are you saying you didn't already do every possible background check when hiring Austin? Did you make a *mistake*, Miss Bennet?" Rosi countered, stepping beside me.

Purple spread across Nicole's cheeks. It was not her color. Her face resembled a giant plum as she spoke quietly and evenly. "The person behind this seems to have a way through those safeguards. I assure you both that challenging me will only result in my finding the truth faster."

"Good. We expect an apology when you find out who did do it," Rosi said, slipping her hand in mine. "When you figure that out, let us know and maybe we can help."

She dragged me from the room with quick steps, head held high until we reached the front of my room again. I ran a hand back through my hair and she twirled a lock of her own, staring back in the direction of Nicole's suite.

"That did not go well," she said.

We both laughed, releasing some of the tension. "I guess my notion you were innocent was flawed by the assumption that I was in the clear."

"Unless you're doing it with your mind powers, I doubt that." Unable to keep from touching her, I rubbed her arms and smiled.

"No mind powers that I know of," she said, refusing to look at me. Was that embarrassment?

"Let's discuss the excursion," I said, gesturing to my room. Why wait until right beforehand after all? If I was worried starting something with her would be bad in my boss's eyes, I no longer had to worry since they already thought much worse of me.

"Okay," she agreed. "I don't want to impose, but Cora has at least two other people in our suite, and if I stay there, they'll try and have sex with me again."

I froze in shock as she continued inside the room and took a seat. If she was going to have sex with someone here, I hoped it would be me. I hurried to catch up and stopped at the kitchen to grab a couple of hydropods. I tossed one to her then sat near her on the couch. She'd already pulled a notebook out of her bag and was scribbling in it.

"The expedition—"

"Excursion," I corrected.

She wrinkled her nose in distaste. "Okay, excursion then, is one day. Is there any way to extend that if we find something?"

I shook my head. "It's four hours. That's all they could get approved for safety reasons. Anything longer would be a logistics nightmare for Nicole."

"And that's a bad thing because..?" Rosi grinned.

Laughing, I leaned back into the cushions. "Seriously. It's officially part of the resort and your prize package."

She tapped her pen to her chin thoughtfully. "Okay so four hours. That's not a lot of time."

Sipping on my water, I waited as she worked it out.

"What we need to do is target a specific area." She stood and walked to the enormous, windowed wall and stared outside. "When I first got here, I thought I saw something out there by the fjord."

I stood and joined her at the window, squinting toward the direction she indicated. The way the light played on the surface of the water and the shadows created by the ice caves nearby made the illusion of movement inevitable. But if she wanted to check it out, I was game.

"We can take the hellipod over it and take a closer look."

"Hellipod?" she asked, head snapping toward me.

"Yes. We go on the hellipod ride to survey the area from above. You get to pick a location, and if I deem it safe, we can land, and you can take vids or whatever you want to do. Then we fly back."

"That's it?" The disappointment radiating off her tugged at my heartstrings. It didn't sound like much to me either. But Nicole had assured me that whoever won the prize wouldn't think that way. She seemed to be wrong about quite a few things.

"Think of it as a scouting mission," I offered, gesturing at her mystery area. "We cover a lot of ground in the hellipod, but we stay thorough. Then we pick the most likely spot to find an *Adlet* and set down there."

Her mouth dropped open. "You know what an *Adlet* is?"

I shrugged. "I looked it up after our talk."

The notebook fell from her grip, and before I could blink, she leaped into my arms.

Stumbling back against the window, I caught hold of her ass as she wrapped her legs around my waist. She pressed against me, and the contrast of the heat coming from her and the cold from the AC glass behind me had all my nerve endings firing at once. Her lips found mine, and I opened to her immediately.

"Condom?" she breathed into my ear.

"I'm on the pill," I answered. "First time in a year. I'm clean."

Then her tongue was in my mouth again, and all thought flew out of my mind except putting one leg in front of the other to get us to my bed.

13

ROSI

HE CARRIED ME TO HIS BED WHERE HE LAY ME GENTLY ON THE mattress and stood to rip off his shirt. I licked my swollen lips as I planned exactly how I was going to explore every one of those ridges in his physique. And when he dropped his pants, and his cock sprung loose, I squeezed my legs together to try and quell the sudden spike of desire.

"Fuck, you are *hot,*" I said in disbelief. And as if he weren't attractive enough, he blushed adorably.

"Your turn," he said, hands on hips.

I felt the grin stretch across my face as I sat up on my knees and peeled off my Mothman T-shirt. Hopefully, he liked the barely there, black bra I'd picked out this morning.

His response came in the form of him grasping me by the waistband and knocking me back on the bed in a fit of giggles. He tugged the jeans from my body, revealing the even skimpier black thong I wore beneath.

Giggles turned to gasps of pleasure as he tugged back the material of my bra to take my nipple in his mouth, circling it with his tongue before sucking and teasing it with his teeth. I grasped handfuls of the sheets as I dragged my hands down the bed, searching for purchase.

Appreciative sounds escaped as he repeated the process with my other breast and slid a hand down my side to the string of material hugging my hip.

"You taste like dessert," he growled, backing away to slip the panties off me.

Responding became impossible when he dove straight for the prize, hooking my knees over his shoulders as he buried his face between my thighs.

Only my shoulders, arms, and head remained on the bed as the stubble I'd imagined last night became reality, awakening every sensitive molecule between my legs. The real thing was a thousand times better than my fantasy as his tongue lapped at the crease of my folds.

"Oh," I gasped as a spasm of pure pleasure washed through me like a wave.

He burrowed deeper, lifting me almost to the point of a headstand as he sucked my clit right into his mouth, making me cry out in pleasure. He pulled at the spot, then circled it with his tongue before slipping back to my core and dipping in and out of me until my legs trembled with the building pressure inside.

"I need more inside of me," I directed, and he set me back on the bed, obeying quickly and thoroughly with his long fingers. He worked them expertly and leaned back down to focus his attention on my clit.

"Oh fuck, Austin," I yelled as my pleasure mounted, skyrocketing me toward release. "Don't stop."

Instead of stopping, he increased his pace and depth, flicking me with his tongue in a punishing rhythm until I clenched every muscle around him in an uncontrollable explosion of ecstasy.

He lifted his head from between my legs and sucked both of his fingers with lust clouding his sexy gray eyes. "Your taste is addictive, Rosi."

That undid me. I shoved him back on the bed so his head was near the footboard and climbed over him. His eyes rolled back as I slid my slick core along his substantial length. Daniel, my dissertation advisor, wasn't nearly as large. Nor was the boyfriend before him. But my body wanted all of Austin inside me, and he was more than ready judging by the way he gripped my ass and grunted.

I worked myself over the tip, taking him in slowly and steadily. Gripping the footboard, I lowered my body down, relishing the way he stretched me, filling me completely until I settled over the entire length of him. *Oh God he felt good inside me.*

He moaned my name as he bucked his hips up, thrusting into me. I threw my head back, hanging on to the footboard like I was riding a wild bull, afraid of being thrown off.

"I need more leverage. You're killing me, Rosi." He lifted me off the bed with him still inside and pressed me up against the wall. I hooked my legs around his back, and he laced his fingers through mine, high above our heads.

"That's better," he said, adjusting his position to pump inside me with fierce abandon. "Tell me if I'm hurting you."

"No," I breathed. "Fuck me harder." He'd found the magical G-spot, and I was ready to come undone all over again.

"So fucking hot," he said as he rocked into me, thudding against the wall with more speed and force until I no longer knew where he started and I ended.

I screamed with the most intense release I'd ever felt, and he continued to thrust into me, desperate for his own climax, which came moments later as I continued to unravel, wondering if the orgasm would ever stop.

But it did, and the feel of him throbbing inside me told me he was still climaxing too.

His mouth covered mine as he pulled out and set me gently on the ground. But he continued the kiss, this time slowly savoring, the kind I could get lost in. And thank goodness he held onto me because I didn't trust that I had my land legs back yet.

Cradling my face, he deepened the kiss, drawing another moan from me before pulling back to survey my reaction. His stormy eyes searched my face for something, but all I could do was stand there, panting, mouth ajar.

His thumb traced my lips before he slipped back to the bed to sit.

"That was amazing." I decided to state the obvious.

But he smiled at me in a way I hadn't seen before. It was kind of...goofy and lopsided. I liked it. A lot.

"Let me know when you're ready to do it again," I said, flipping my crazy hair from my face and sitting beside him.

"I could do this all night, Rosi. Be careful what you wish for."

The soreness had already bloomed between my thighs, but maybe if we tried it a bit more slowly this time...

My wristband buzzed, and Cora's name flashed across the screen.

"What?" I asked, choosing to use audio only or risk being teased for the rest of my life.

"Are you okay?" she asked, sending my pulse into panic mode.

"Yeah, why? What happened now?"

"Thank God. Sherri and I left the room to pick up some food, and by the time we got back we'd nearly frozen to death! The climate controls outside of the rooms changed to match the outside temps. Now we're in emergency lockdown mode, and everyone's trapped inside their rooms unless they bundle up and move fast. How have you not heard this yet?"

Exchanging a glance with Austin, we both jumped off the bed. "We haven't tried to go out."

"Well trust me, you shouldn't."

Austin rushed out to the front of the suite butt naked and pressed his palms to the door. Jumping back quickly with a yelp and wide eyes, he looked at me. Damn, even in this situation I had to pause to appreciate the perfection of his ass.

"Right. Does maintenance know?"

"Duh." I imagined Cora cocking a hip and tossing her hair. "I called them first thing when I got back to the room. They're working on it. I just wanted to check on you because I hadn't heard from you."

"I'm okay. At least we have everything we need inside the suite."

"Wait. How could I have been so blind? I bet you *do* have everything in there. No wonder you haven't come out or called. So how is he in bed?"

Before I could suffer any more embarrassment, I disconnected the call with a quick, "Gotta go."

At least the rooms were still livable. Things could have been worse than being trapped with Austin for a few days.

14

ROSI

"WE SHOULD GET DRESSED IN CASE ANYONE COMES TO CHECK ON US," Austin suggested with one hand caressing my breast.

I took his shaft in my hand and stroked it lightly in response.

"Sex under risk of discovery sounds like an extreme sport to me," I said.

He squeezed my breast and twisted my nipple between his fingers, making me squeak before muffling the sound with his mouth.

This was our third round of sex, and his stamina was inspiring. My body was exhausted but seemed to wake up and respond every time he touched me. The second time he'd taken me as I lay across the kitchen counter and he stood at the end, sliding me toward him and spearing me with his cock. It was incredible. Neither of my previous lovers had any imagination when it came to positioning.

This time we were back on the bed, and I pictured something a bit more standard. That was until he flipped me over and asked me to get on my knees. Based on the new pleasures I'd experienced during the last couple of rounds, I decided to comply.

"Don't bend over, sit up while kneeling." He guided my legs apart and meshed his body along my back so I could feel his cock ready once again, slipping against the slickness of my folds from behind.

I reached back to grasp his neck as he leaned his head over my shoulder, meeting me for a kiss. One of his hands toyed with my breasts and the other wandered down my stomach and in between my legs to find my clit.

I gasped as he pressed on it, circling it roughly with his finger while his tongue slid inside my mouth. Then his cock eased inside me from behind. He thrust in and out of me as our bodies undulated together in a dance he controlled.

He swallowed every exclamation I made with his never-ending kiss, and I marveled at his ability to focus on so many moving parts. If he hadn't been supporting me, I'd have been jelly on the mattress.

My climax came and went and came again as he built toward his own. I feared I'd pass out before he got there, but instead I clenched around him as he pressed against my nub, coming undone as though on command.

He answered with his own moan, holding me in place as he emptied himself yet again.

"Fuck," he said as he lowered us both to the bed. "You are amazing."

If I had any words left, I'd assure him of the same. And if nothing else happened on this vacation, I'd had the best sex of my life. There was nowhere to go from here in that department, I was certain.

He spooned against me, cradling my body in a way that made me feel completely secure, and I allowed myself to drift off in his arms, certain no nightmares could find me with his protection.

When I woke, it was to Austin kissing my cheek.

I stretched and smiled up at him buttoning his shirt and couldn't decide whether to be happy or upset that he was dressed.

"What time is it?" I asked.

"You slept through the night. It's 9 a.m. standard time, and they

fixed the climate issues while we slept. Nicole has a press conference planned and asked me to be there. You can stay here if you
want."

"I'll come too," I offered, sitting up.

"I'd love that. But it's in five minutes, and I suspect it might take
you longer to get ready."

"That's a very macho assumption," I said, getting out of the bed
and stumbling to the bathroom, determined to prove him wrong.
But when I caught sight of my reflection, I swore under my breath.
"*Mierda.*"

It wasn't just that I had the fresh-fucked look of impossibly
messy hair. My face had what appeared like rugburn all along my
chin, and a dark bruises bloomed on either side of my neck and at
my collar bone. I wondered if there was a similar mark between my
legs as well.

"Thanks, Austin," I said a bit louder.

"Sorry!" he called before I heard the doors *woosh* shut.

He was right. It'd take a bit of makeup to hide the hickies and
burn marks from his stubble. Resigned to taking a shower and
getting myself in order, I started the process. The reality of having
spent almost an entire afternoon and evening fucking Austin
Cooper set in sometime between applying shampoo and condi-
tioner, and I laughed out loud.

When I finished showering and turned on the instadryer, I
started thinking more about my conversation with Ila. So, her
family had spiritual connections. That thing in the glass case was
from her great-grandfather, and he'd—if I'd understood what I
read—carved it from actual bone, possibly the bones of one of the
monster's victims and then masturbated over it. I tried to keep a no-
judgement policy, but that felt fucked up. Had the little statue actually come to life and found the guy and killed him? According to
the legends, if it hadn't, that meant it would've come back and
killed Ila's great-grandad. Surely, she'd have mentioned if that had
happened.

After airbrushing some makeup over my new blemishes with the standard makeup machine found in all the suites, I surveyed my much-improved reflection. Even my curls seemed to be under control for once.

I went into Austin's living area and turned on the holo.

"Computer, show me the press conference from Glacial Palace Resort."

The 3-D image popped in front of me. Nicole looked as perfect as ever as she stood on the podium with a smile.

"Yes, we immediately took the AI offline and thoroughly checked for any code that didn't belong. It's clean. We also thoroughly checked for unapproved tech. Also clean." She pointed at someone in the audience.

"The vid that went viral of Austin Cooper doing that free fall stunt with the hover disks? Was that an accident or a separate stunt?" asked one of the journalists.

Nicole motioned for Austin to step forward from the shadows, and I instantly recognized his fake smile as lights flashed around him in the frenzy of bots that flew around his head. He waved.

"That was a rehearsed stunt I talked the contest winner, Rosalind Sanchez, into doing with me." He chuckled, and the reporters laughed with him.

My face burned. Why was he lying? Had Nicole talked him into that to try to distract from the real issues? It had to be her, leveraging her theory about us being saboteurs against him, so he had no choice.

"How is Ms. Sanchez?" someone asked.

"I'm making sure she has the time of her life. And I never do things half-assed." Austin winked at the cameras.

He fucking winked.

Before I knew what I was doing, I'd stood up in the center of the holo and stalked toward him like I could actually reach out and slap him.

"Where is she?" a familiar voice asked. I spun around, searching for the source and then remembered it was the same voice that asked me to find out—

"I want to ask if she knows yet whether you have boxers or tighty-whities."

That one.

Austin shook his head, blushing and grinning like an idiot. "Let's just say I don't think she paid much attention to what I was wearing last I saw her."

Starting to hyperventilate, I shouted at the holo to pause. Then I tried to get control of my runaway brain because it wanted to march down there and find Austin so I could murder him.

"It's all an act," I said out loud. But I wasn't very convincing, especially after being intimate with him. Still, he had some sort of sponsorship he depended on them for, he'd said. I supposed it wasn't like he'd given any details.

Pretending I wasn't hurt but having evened out my breathing, I said, "Continue holo."

I crossed my arms over my chest like armor as I watched Austin waggle his eyebrows and point to someone else in the crowd.

"Where is the contest winner?" someone asked.

"Trying to stay calm," I answered.

"She and I had a...busy night." Austin paused for a bout of laughter as my heart stopped.

"Helping her study?" some idiot journalist commented with a snort.

"Studying physiology," Austin said and winked again.

"Computer, shut off holo."

Tears burned my eyes as I stomped to my own room. I was in no mood to see another moment. No wonder he hadn't woken me early enough to get ready to join him. It was one thing to bend the truth to make the resort look good, but that stuff about me was completely unnecessary. It was my reputation being smeared, and now all over the world people thought of me as some sort of starstruck slut who couldn't string a sentence together. Nicole might appreciate the distraction, but this was my life we were talking about. I thought I'd meant something more than a one-night stand to Austin. But what did I really know about his intentions?

At the very least, I'd never imagined he would embarrass me on television.

I stormed into my suite, and Cora looked up from the sofa. I thanked the Fates she was dressed and alone.

"If there's anyone else in here they have to the count of three to get the fuck out," I announced.

"No one. They're getting ready for a show tonight," Cora said. "What happened?"

"Computer, replay holo of the press conference. The part where Austin Cooper speaks."

I sank onto one of the massage pods and let it play for Cora, who threw a hand over her mouth in response. When it ended she said, "Shit."

"Yeah, thanks for tossing me to the *adlets*," I said, lying backward and letting my head hang upside down off the cushion.

"I'm so sorry. That was not what I saw in the cards."

"Well maybe your cards were wrong, chica."

She glared at me.

I shouldn't have said it. I knew how sensitive she was about others not believing in her. But this wasn't about her. It was about me trusting the wrong person. Again. He probably didn't even believe me, just pretended to so I'd fuck him. It was my own damn fault for getting all gooey-eyed over the first guy to act like he understood me. That was how desperate I was.

Cora grabbed my hands and tugged me up into a sitting position. "My cards are never wrong. That"—she pointed at the spot the holo had been—"was the lie. Not whatever happened between you."

Tears stung my eyes as I tried to make sense of it logically. How could I reconcile what I'd just seen with the Austin I thought I'd gotten to know? It had only been a few days. How could I really *know* someone in that amount of time?

I stuffed a curl in my mouth and chewed as Cora's face blurred behind the tears that filled my eyes. A realization hit me like a boulder on the head. The last fifteen years of my life I'd dedicated to uncovering the truth. But I'd done it to force others to believe in *me*, not the monsters. That sasquatch didn't *want* to be discovered. It'd disappeared into the woods as fast as it could for privacy. I was the one forcing the issue. No wonder no one had real evidence yet. Not only did they not want to be found, but the world didn't want to find them. I was the only one fucked up enough to try and change that.

"What's happening in that head of yours?" Cora asked, sitting cross-legged in front of me.

"I just had an epiphany," I said, sniffling.

"You realized that Austin was just acting for the cameras and Nicole because it's his job?" she asked, brushing the hair from my face.

I shook my head and whimpered. "No. I realized that this whole time, what I've been wanting is someone to believe in me."

"Oh, honey, I believe in you." She flung her arms wide, and I fell into her hug.

Sobs wracked my body as she rocked me like a baby. When the sobbing stopped producing actual tears, I coughed and straightened up, blinking at Cora's smiling face.

"Tissues," I said through my stuffy nose.

She reached over and snatched some from the arm of the couch. I didn't ask why they were there, just yanked out a handful and blew my nose while she waited.

"I don't know what I'd do without you," I said.

"Same," she answered. "How are you feeling?"

How was I feeling? Thoroughly fucked in more ways than one.

"Like I should take a break from Austin Cooper." I straightened my spine. "I got too invested. I need to focus on my work and look at the last twenty-four hours the same way Austin obviously is—like nothing more than a little fun and a way to get what I want."

Cora sighed as I finished standing.

"Why are you so determined to match me up with Austin anyway? I thought you just wanted me to loosen up and have some fun. Well, I did. So be happy and let it go."

"I'm not trying to force you into anything," she said, palms out. "And for the record, I'm glad you had fun. I'm sorry that he hurt you, but I also think everything happens for a reason, and maybe, just maybe, you figuring something out about yourself was exactly that."

I pursed my lips to prevent myself from responding in anger. She was trying to help. I stole a page from Austin's book and took a deep breath.

"Okay, fine. It wasn't pleasant, but you're right. I did learn something," I said, moving to the kitchen to order some coffee. And as I sipped, an idea popped in my head. "Get your cards out, chica, I have some questions."

15

AUSTIN

IT DIDN'T TAKE A ROCKET SCIENTIST TO FIGURE OUT THAT ROSI watched the press conference. Maybe part of me wanted her to, so she'd see what an ass I really was. It worked. Not a single comm had come from her all week, and we didn't so much as run in to each other in the halls. Though to be fair, I'd been hiding in my suite most of that time. Since the anti-grav track proved detrimental to my health and wellbeing, I decided to work with yoga and various free weights here. Nicole ordered me a climbing machine as well, which came in handy, moving like an old-fashioned stair climber but changing footholds in all directions at increasing time intervals.

Having finished with my cardio, I started my stretches, but my mind refused to quiet. Rosi was all I could think about. Her beautiful smile, the sounds she made while we fucked, her sugary taste...

I climbed the wall with my bare feet until I stood with my hands and balanced, holding the pose. I'd gotten the distance I wanted, so why was I so miserable? That night with her should've been enough to hold me over for another full year of focus without sex. Maybe it was too good. Maybe I was addicted to her body. It had to be her body because I wasn't willing to accept the idea of being addicted to her soul. Relationships were not something that fit in my lifestyle.

Feelings were not something that fit in my lifestyle. And she'd provoked too many of them—more than I'd allowed myself in the last five years.

"Fuck." I let my legs fall over and squatted upright. Grabbing my hydropod, I squeezed the remainder into my dry mouth and finished it. One thing was for certain, she'd gotten in my head and disrupted my ability to focus.

At least there hadn't been any more tech issues since the press conference.

Breathe, I demanded, sitting in a lotus position.

In, two, three, four...

Why can't I get her out of my head?

The wrinkled face of Tenzin Yeshe Rinpoche appeared in my mind with a look that said, "You are not focused."

I'm trying, Lama.

"We must first release what troubles us before we can be free."

Trust me, I've released her. She wouldn't come near me again if I begged.

My teacher's lips turned down ever so slightly as he shook his head. *Not bury or run.* Release. *Each experience is a lesson. You are refusing your lesson. Now focus.*

The words rang in my brain as my eyes popped open. I let out a frustrated sigh. I wished I could speak to the real Rinpoche, not just the one in my head, but it wasn't like I could fly to Tibet and back before tomorrow's excursion. Part of me hoped Rosi'd cancel it and refuse to be near me. But I knew that was wishful thinking—or according to my own mind—avoidance thinking. Rosi would never give up her plans to search for evidence of cryptids just to avoid me. She was driven, and I appreciated that about her.

A hot shower would help, I decided and relaxed the moment the warmth hit my muscles. Then for the hundredth time, I wondered what she'd been up to for the past days. Had she thought of me?

"Aaarrgh!" I rubbed my hands over my face, splattering water. Why did it matter if I wanted to avoid her? Not that another night or four of mind-blowing sex wouldn't be welcome, but the feels I'd started to get were a huge no-no. That would only lead to complications and trouble and...what if it ended like it had with Sara?

The sudden burst of cold water made me jump from the shower and slide across the floor a good foot. *What the fuck?* I hadn't allowed myself to think of that name in almost five years without my guard up, and then the hot water shut off the moment I did?

Standing soaking wet and naked in the bathroom, I froze. There hadn't been an incident since the press conference. Every single thing that had happened did so when I was around, specifically when I had a big emotional response I couldn't control. I'd gone to Tibet for the first time after Sara had drowned, and the monks, especially Tenzin Yeshe, had helped me through the mourning process by teaching me meditation and other techniques. And it had worked wonders until—

Until I met Rosi.

My laugh echoed in the small shower cavern. "Don't be a dumb-ass, Austin." There was no way what I'd been thinking was possible, that I'd held in my energy and now it was powerful enough to affect the tech around me. I wasn't Buddha—did he have that ability? I didn't think so...

Turning off the shower, I decided to get dressed and go for a walk. Maybe I'd find something to distract myself. Whether it really was me causing the issues or not, the last thing I wanted was for more thoughts of Sara to surface. When it came to her, I had no doubts who was at fault.

16

ROSI

CORA *HAD* TO PULL THE TOWER. NOT THAT I WAS AN EXPERT, BUT I knew the worst card in the deck when I saw it. She tried to put some sort of spin on it, like "Sometimes something has to happen in order to clear space for what you need and yadda yadda yadda."

I appreciated the effort, but the concern in her eyes shoved me over the edge. I got up and went to lie in bed for the next day, refusing to let her pull any more cards, especially when she tried to tell me the Lovers came next. Disaster followed by the Lovers did not make me feel better.

"Tomorrow's the big day, are you ready?" Cora asked, studiously ignoring the bowl of ice cream in my hands.

Flicking off the holos, I shoved a bite of rocky road in my mouth as I stared back at her.

Cora cocked a hip and tossed her hair. "You're going."

"You can go. Tell me if you find anything," I said, mushing the mounds of chocolaty goodness until they started to melt.

"Fuck that," Cora said. "Your whole life revolves around this obsession of yours and you are going tomorrow, or you'll regret it."

I opened my mouth to respond, pointing the spoon at her, but she continued over me.

"Do not let a man prevent you from being you."

My mouth snapped shut. She was right, damn her. Austin might've crushed my expectations, but he was the asshole here, not me. I set the bowl on the floor for the cleaning bots and stood up.

"Fine. We're going on that excursion tomorrow, and Austin Cooper is going to take us exactly where I tell him to."

"That's my Rosi!" Cora said, clapping. "Let's get you packed."

"I've had my backpack packed for this trip since we arrived," I admitted. "Let's go check out the dog sleds instead. I've been wanting a chance to get out there."

Cora agreed, and we both dressed in the thermal clothing we'd purchased for the trip, including socks, pants, and sweaters. We then piled on our parkas, gloves, scarves, and thermal face shields before zipping into our boots. We looked like, well, like were about to go check out some dog sleds.

When we made it through the double set of doors to the exit, the biting cold hit the bits of skin at the edges of my thermals, the line between my neck and scarf and my wrists and sleeves. The force of the wind howled as it rushed over us, shoving us back a few steps as though trying to stop us from venturing out of the resort. But the rosy-cheeked family that rushed past us on their way back in told me it was worth the fight, and with Cora holding tightly to my arm, we made it to the now empty *qamutik* where a young Inuk man, who looked no older than my own twenty-five years, adjusted the straps over a beautiful white husky.

Next to him stood a shorter, familiar figure with a thick gray parka and round face.

"Hi, Ila!" I greeted her as several other dogs gathered round us, curious. "This is my friend, Cora."

"Hello, Cora," Ila yelled over the wind. "This is my son, Toklo. He takes care of the dogs."

That explained why she was out here. "Hi, Toklo, nice to meet you. I'm Rosi. I had no idea you had a son working here, Ila."

Ila grinned. "That wasn't one of your questions."

"You here for a ride?" Toklo asked, releasing the dog whose harness he'd been adjusting then giving it a brisk rub on the head. The dog barked. "Yuka wants me to introduce you."

"Hello, Yuka," I said, reaching down to let him sniff my glove before patting him.

The other dogs crowded in and ran around us, begging to play. Cora dropped to her knees in the crunchy snow and began petting as many as she could.

"We'd love a ride if it's not too hard on the dogs," I said.

Toklo shrugged. "They seem to want more exercise. I never ride them too hard. It's just for fun anyway. Not like we need these things anymore with hover tech."

He reminded me of his mother, practical yet knowledgeable in the traditions of his people. "Sounds good then. Want to join us, Ila?"

"Nah. There's a cabana by the pool with my name on it. But you enjoy yourselves. Good thing you came today." Ila glanced up at the sky, shielding her eyes. "Clear now, but there's a snowstorm headed in in the next day or two."

"I hope not," I said, exchanging a look with Cora. "My expedition is scheduled for tomorrow, and I don't want to cancel it."

"It'll probably wait until at least tomorrow night," Ila assured me.

"Can you feel it?" Cora asked, eyes wide as a dog jumped to lick her face.

Ila laughed. "Nah. The weather service announced it. They have some control these days, but it's best to let nature take its course when it isn't causing major issues."

"Come on ladies, meet the dogs before we go. You know Yuka, and that's Anjij, Aput, Asiaq, Siqiniq, and Kalik."

There was no way in hell I could keep straight who was who, but their joy and playfulness made me feel so much better. It made me wish I'd been out here every day.

Toklo expertly hitched the dogs up to what looked like a traditional sled with thick slats set across it to sit on. Waterproof blankets piled over it, looking inviting, and an area at the front had two vertical slats about hip-width apart and handles for someone to grab hold of when steering. I estimated he could easily take a family of four for a ride around the ice fields outside the resort.

Toklo told us more about the dogs as he worked.

"My people bred them from wolves," he explained.

"They're so playful," Cora said, surprise written on her face when she looked up from rubbing Yuka's belly.

Within minutes we were loaded onboard, swathed in blankets, Cora behind me and Toklo driving. He lowered his goggles and asked, "Where to, ladies? The small hill to the right or the circular area to the left?"

"Can we go toward the fjord?" I asked, sudden inspiration hitting. I pointed out where I'd seen something moving that first day we checked in.

The difference in Toklo's posture and expression when I asked was obvious even through all the layers of gear and protection. "Too far and I don't want the dogs breaking through the ice."

"How about the rocky part to the right of it? The one that looks like caves?" I yelled over the wind that had picked up again.

I shivered right through my layers of warmth as he seemed to do some sort of internal debate.

"What's wrong?" I asked.

"The dogs don't like it over there," he answered. "But I haven't tried in a week or so, and I guess it wouldn't hurt to head that way and see if they've changed their minds."

I smiled and gave a double thumbs up as excitement rose in my belly. The dogs had reacted to something. Maybe it was the same something I'd seen with my binoculars.

Cora grabbed hold of me as we lurched forward into a race across the white tundra. The feeling was unlike anything I'd ever experienced, though it reminded me of sledding with Austin to escape the drones. I pushed that thought aside, telling myself this was ten times the feeling, with so much open space to explore and the dogs powering the ride.

The rocky formation grew larger as we drew closer, the clear waters of the fjord reflecting the light of the lowering sun. Pockets of ice floated along the surface, and I appreciated why he wouldn't want the dogs to try to go on it. I reached for my pack and fished out the binoculars, letting them clasp to my face as I searched the rocks and shadows to the right of the fjord. The dogs weren't reacting, so I wondered if that meant whatever I'd seen had moved on.

Then the wind picked up again, racing over us from the direction of the resort with an ear-piercing howl. The sled swayed, and the dogs jolted to the left in a cacophony of howls, barks, and whines.

Toklo stumbled to the side but sunk his weight onto one foot. He held tight to the handle as the dogs pulled us in a complete U-turn so fast the sled tipped to the side as well. Cora and I screamed in unison.

Grabbing for anything I could get a hold of, I ended up on my stomach, foot hanging off the sled. I tilted my head as far as I could to look behind us at the rapidly shrinking rocks I'd gotten so close to and noticed a shadow pulling quickly back toward the rocks. It moved like a spider, scurrying, and far too fast to be from the sinking sunlight.

The movement stopped suddenly, and not at all naturally as Toklo regained control of the sled and we slowed to a stop. I scrambled to a sitting position again, staring back out at the too-still area, waiting for something to happen. My eyes burned from keeping them from blinking lest I miss something.

Cora groaned, and I tore my gaze from the search to find her lying on her side, one hand over her head, dark crimson slipping through her fingers.

"She's bleeding!" I yelled back to Toklo as I leaned over my friend, prying her hand away to take a look at the wound.

It appeared she'd banged her head on the edge of the sled when we were jerked around in the opposite direction. Logically, I knew head wounds bled a lot, but seeing it was a whole different situation.

"We have to get her back to the resort," Toklo said. "Keep pressure on it and keep her as steady as you can. I'll call ahead for medical help."

I crawled around behind Cora and pulled her head and shoulders in my lap just as the sled sprung into motion again. I used a blanket to put pressure on the wound and begged her to stay conscious. Minutes ticked by like hours.

A hovercot waited for us at the entrance to the double set of doors, and Toklo pulled us as close as possible to the building. I watched as two people lifted Cora gently onto the floating stretcher. They held up a hand when I attempted to follow.

"Let us get her inside and stabilized. You can meet us in the medcenter," said the redheaded doctor I recognized from my short stay after Austin's fall from the tube.

I nodded numbly and glanced back toward the sled, where Toklo had released the dogs, who ran and jumped as though nothing strange had happened. Shaking my head and hugging myself, I looked back toward the rocks and touched my temple to zoom in with the binoculars I still wore.

A gray blur disappeared in the shadowed alcove of rocks in the farthest corner from the fjord. I could have almost sworn it had been waiting there, watching. Chills raced over me.

What the fuck was that?

17

ROSI

"Hey, are you okay?"

I jumped when Toklo set a hand on my shoulder. He jerked it back.

"Yeah. That was…" I couldn't find the word.

"What? You didn't know it was supposed to be a thrill ride?" Toklo smiled, and I appreciated his valiant attempt at getting me to laugh.

"There was something back there. Something that scared the dogs," I said, yanking off the binoculars. That blur had moved so quickly then disappeared. It would have made even me question whether I'd actually seen something, except for the dogs' reactions.

Toklo's sparkling grin melted. He shoved his gloved hands in his coat pockets and frowned at Yuka, who sat before him, tongue lolling. "Yeah. I'm sorry I agreed to try it again. I thought maybe whatever spooked them was temporary. *Anaq, anaqsitaumni.*"

I didn't speak Inuktitut, but I got the gist. He blamed himself.

"It wasn't your fault. I asked to go there when you gave me two very enjoyable options. The truth is I thought I saw something there before and wanted to check it out. This is on me." Cora's *injury* was on me.

"You saw something?" Toklo's gaze shot toward me, and Yuka whined. "What did you see?"

I shifted, making the snow crunch beneath me. This was the point where people typically laughed or rolled their eyes. But something in Toklo's demeanor told me he might actually react differently. And if he did, that would make this particular thing... real. While the sasquatch had frightened me, it had been gentle and wanted to be alone. This—whatever it was, did not have as nice of a vibe.

"I don't know," I answered truthfully. "Movement, but more than shadow and light. It had substance." I glanced back out at the area, now so far away and yet too close. Suddenly, I wanted to get inside and find Cora.

"Well, I won't be taking the dogs down there again." Toklo squatted to pet Yuka while looking off in the same direction.

"What do you think it is?" I lowered my voice as I, too, knelt to pet the dog.

Toklo's oaken eyes met mine. "It could be any number of things. Hopefully, just an animal. But if you grew up with my dad, you'd be thinking more along the lines of a *qallupilluk*."

I knew the term. I'd studied the myths. It was basically the bogeyman of the water, waiting to drag children beneath the ice. I shivered. Growing up in San Diego, I'd heard stories of *la llarona*, my culture's equivalent.

"I better get inside and see how Cora's doing," I said, squeezing Toklo's puffy sleeve and giving Yuka one last pat.

"Yeah, I think we're done for the day. I'm gonna get the dogs inside."

"Nice to meet you, Toklo," I said as I headed for the double doors.

Suddenly, even the ultra-tough AC glass felt too thin for comfort.

18

AUSTIN

"You wanted to see me?"

Jackson stepped back from the door, and Nicole ushered me inside with the wave of her hand. She was seated at the table with her holopads again and barely glanced up as I approached.

"Yes. The excursion is tomorrow."

"Yes it is," I replied, still annoyed that she'd asked me to behave that way for the press conference. I was an athlete, not an actor, and I didn't appreciate head games. The only reason I did it was to make sure Rosi knew I wasn't worth her time. She deserved a lot more than what I could offer, and it was the only way to keep her away from me because I when I was near her, I had no fucking self-control.

At this point Nicole looked up and swiveled toward me. Her ice-blue eyes seemed to cut straight through to my brain. "If anything happens on that outing other than holo vids and a ride over the scenery, I will have you confined to quarters for the remainder of the trip and arrested on return to the mainland. Is that understood?"

Heat rushed to my cheeks, but I breathed through it without

pause. I felt bad for people like Nicole. People whose lives centered around always being on the defensive, afraid of attack, who were focused on the wrong things. But I didn't want to pay for her insecurities with my career.

"I am not a saboteur. I thought we'd been over this," I said, simply tired of dealing with it.

Nicole smiled. She was gorgeous, but she did nothing for me. We were very different people.

"Of course. I'm just covering my bases. Whatever she offered you that you thought you couldn't get from me, well, it won't do you any good in prison." She went back to her holopads in silent dismissal.

"She?" I asked, curious.

"Whoever is behind this ridiculous attempt to shut down the Fantasy Resorts," Nicole snapped. "He, she, they, it. I don't care what my enemy's pronouns are. Just make a good choice when you take those women out for the excursion. And let Ms. Sanchez know that whatever you two have planned is off the table. In fact, just so you know, no one is going to be aware you're out there. Not until it's over."

"But you said it would be broadcast live across the—" I protested, knowing that was part of the marketing.

"There will be a recorder for both of you, and we will edit the footage later. The date is four days from now according to all advertising and scheduling materials as of a week ago. So if you do try to pull something, no one will see it or know about it. Just me."

Inhaling, I swallowed back my next remark. She could live with her suspicions. Nothing was going to happen on the excursion. Rosi would look for her cryptids, and we'd go back to the resort and part ways. End of story. End of whatever it was that might have been between us.

The lights blinked overhead, and Nicole and I glanced up at the same time.

"If you'll excuse me, I have to speak to Ms. Sanchez about the details." I forced a smile and left the suite. Nicole could worry about how I magically did that if she wanted to waste her time. I had more agonizing conversations to deal with.

But contacting Rosi proved impossible. I thought she'd have answered at least to go over the details. I hoped I hadn't hurt her that badly with the press conference. There was no way her feelings for me ran that deep, was there?

Early the next morning, I showed up outside the double doors of the resort exit where the hellipod waited, a spherical contraption with a rotating propellor on top. I half expected Rosi not to turn up after all, but there she was, walking toward me across the glinting surface of the ground. She was covered in gear and all the appropriate clothing, but my cock reacted at the memory of the last time we were together. At least it wouldn't be obvious with all the layers I wore.

"Where's your friend?" A puff of steam released along with my words.

"She was injured yesterday. She's okay, but she's staying in. Let's go while the weather is good." Rosi turned her back to me and climbed in the automated hellipod, ducking below the propellor.

My heart sunk. This was going to be a torturous four hours. *You deserve it, you ass,* I told myself as I climbed in after her. The AC glass doors slid closed, blocking out the cold and leaving us in sudden silence with a 360-degree view. The bench seat circled the entire pod. She sat at the farthest point from the door, arms and legs crossed. I sat near the door, respecting her space for fear of being torn to shreds, and pulled off my ski mask.

"Rosi, I—"

"Don't," she said, also pulling off her mask. I wish she hadn't because seeing the hurt in her chocolate eyes and knowing I put it there, made me wince.

"Okay," I said, hanging my head. "Computer, activate hellipod. Take us on preapproved course A."

The hellipod lifted into the air and swayed slightly as it adjusted to our weight and its preprogrammed course. The insides were sparse save for a snack cabinet and an emergency medical supply cabinet beneath the bench.

I snuck a glance at Rosi, but she was looking out the window. In that moment, I desperately wished I had the ability to read her mind.

Below us, Greenland's unabashed beauty unfolded in a dream-scape of white hills, crystal waters, and sunshine that glinted off the entire reflective field to the point I had to squint even through the treated windows. My heart caught in my throat when I realized my first impulse was to put an arm around Rosi and share the experience with her. Seeing the excitement in her eyes, the way they sparkled when she told me about her work, that was what I craved more than anything. And I one hundred percent blew it.

"I'm the biggest idiot in the world," I said, gaze now fixed on Rosi.

She turned to face me, eyebrows raised in challenge.

"Rosi, I can't stop thinking about you. I agreed to help Nicole with her farce of a news conference, but everything I said was idiotic."

"What I just heard: Rosi, I can't stop thinking with my dick, so now I regret being an asshole."

I fell to my knees before her as the hellipod jolted slightly. "I deserve that and more. But it's not my dick that's suffering, it's my heart."

"Wow," she said with a bitter laugh. She looked up at the ceiling of the pod, eyes shining with unshed tears. At least I knew she felt something too. Then she started slowly clapping.

Swallowing back the rush of hurt, I grasped her hands in mine, making her stop and pay attention. She didn't pull away as the hellipod tilted west to come around for another scan of the area.

"There's got to be something I can do to prove I mean it."

"Why'd you do it if you really feel that way? Didn't you tell me you were on my side? That I could trust you?" she asked, sarcasm gone and pain in its place.

I winced and made a decision in that moment. I chose to try to fix things with Rosi, knowing it might be too late, and knowing I was being selfish. But I couldn't stop thinking about her. Step one was to answer her questions.

"Why did I do it? Two reasons. First, I was scared that Nicole wouldn't honor our deal because she thought I was some sort of spy."

"You hurt me, Austin. You deliberately made a fool out of me. You could have ruined my reputation—my career. So, you have one last chance. What's the other reason?" She bit her lip, waiting.

I hesitated. She was right and deserved the truth. But I hadn't said it out loud in years, and it was harder to admit than I thought it would be. I settled on a vague compromise, hoping it would be enough.

"I wanted to scare you off for your own good."

Rosi scoffed yet didn't pull away from my hands. "What makes you think it's for my own good? Don't I get to decide that, *pendejo*?"

"Of course you do! I just...I've hurt people, okay? It's not safe to be with me like that!" I stood and yanked my hand away and shoved it through my hair, pacing and trying to breathe but finding it hard to get air.

The pod lurched, pulling to the side. It dumped my ass on the bench and Rosi on top of me with a scream. I held her tightly around the waist as my head cleared and my training went into gear, commanding me to assess the situation and take control. Judging from the angle and force, the pod was going down.

I cradled Rosi in an attempt to take some of the impact and

found myself centimeters from her, swathed in her vanilla scent. The chances of survival were iffy, and all the training I had told me to focus on our position. But if I was about to die, there was only one thing I wanted.

So I kissed her.

19

ROSI

THE WORLD TURNED UPSIDE DOWN, LITERALLY. WE WERE IN FREE fall, and somehow Austin had a hold of me. I opened my mouth to scream again, and his tongue swept inside—hot, desperate, and savage. The kiss left me dizzier than the plummeting hellipod. Everything he'd been trying to say went into the physical act. I felt his passion, despair, and anguish as completely as I'd ever felt my own. And I kissed him back, sucking, biting, and sloppy as tears ran down my face. Then he pulled back, held my head and looked at me, eyes searching for forgiveness.

I needed to know who he'd hurt that made him so afraid of getting close but realized I might never have that chance. Before I could tell him I forgave him, we crashed.

Blinding white burst over the entire surface of the interior as airbags exploded around us. The pain was everywhere at once as our bodies bounced around the spherical pod like we'd been shoved in a clothes dryer and put on speed dry. Austin's body held tightly to mine, taking the brunt of the force each time we smashed into surprisingly hard surfaces. His hands protected my head, yet the jarring was still so intense my vision shook along with my brain. When it finally stopped, I was sobbing on top of him, clawing at his chest, and he'd released his hold.

After a minute of not moving, I raised my head to assess the damage. Austin lay spread out beneath me, unmoving, pale, and unconscious. I shook his jacket, screamed his name, but he didn't respond.

"No. No, no, no, no, no." I climbed over him, yanking the glove from my hand despite the cold air coming in from some leak or another. I shoved my fingers against his pulse point. *Please be okay*, I silently begged him.

It took a moment to find it, but it was there, a slow thump that pressed back against my fingers. He was alive.

I shoved my glove back on and scrambled around the space, now resembling more of a padded cell in which someone had set off a bomb. I located our balaclavas, dark against the white background. His backpack was trapped beneath an inflated bag and a portion of what had been the bench. I yanked mine loose from where it had caught on the ragged remains of shredded white material covering the snack bin. It was salvageable. We might need those snacks now, so I took the remains of material aside and pulled out as many hydropods as possible before shoving them in my sack.

"Computer," I called as I worked. "Can you get us back to the resort?"

A high-pitched screech made me wince before the soft female voice came from all around. "Negative. The engine is damaged. Calling for emergency backup."

"Thank heaven," I said, sitting back on my knees. "Tell them someone is injured. Maybe badly." I bit back the tears as I chewed on a stray curl sticking out of my hastily replaced mask.

"Unable to contact resort. Communications function no longer accessible."

"There has to be something you can do in case of emergency," I said, checking Austin over for obvious injuries. When I rolled him over to his side, I found the beginnings of a goose-egg on the back of his skull. What was it with me and my friends getting head injuries?

"Medical supply cabinet open," said the computer. "Emergency backup systems unavailabbbbbbllllle."

Great. I scavenged for bandages and cleansing supplies and soon had Austin's head wrapped up like he was part mummy. I swept all the pressure injectors available into my bag except for one stimulant. At least I'd have all the pain meds and anti-inflammatories I could ever want. The sun was low on the horizon, and I needed Austin's expertise if we were going to survive in the arctic.

"Sorry," I told him before depressing the button of the stimulant into his neck. The hiss of the meds deploying filled the pod, and I waited, holding my breath until his head lolled to one side then the other.

Wincing, he sat up too fast and cupped the back of his head with his hand. "Ow."

"Take it easy," I said. "We crashed, and you've been hurt."

"I can tell," he said with another gasp as he righted himself completely. "Are you okay?"

Was I? I took stock and nodded.

He leaned toward me and immediately winced.

"What can I do?" I asked, stopping short of grabbing his arm for fear of making it worse.

"Any RR injectors by chance?" he asked, rolling his shoulder and grimacing. "It's not broken, but I need to be able to move and carry supplies if need be."

I dug in my bag and handed one of the Rapid Recovery pressure injectors to him with trembling hands. I should've done that first. Judging by the tension around his eyes, he was hiding quite a bit of pain. I was terrible at this.

"Hey, it's okay," he said, taking it from me. He injected himself with a cringe and held my shaking hand. "We're alive. We made it through the most dangerous part. The rest will be easy."

But his grin was the one he used on the news vids, and not the real one. Still, I wanted to believe him, and it wouldn't do either of us any good if I freaked out.

"You did great, Rosi. Thank you." He squeezed my hand and got to his knees.

"Thanks. The computer said no engine, no communication, no emergency backup system," I reported.

"Normally, next step would be to scavenge for supplies," he said, eyeing his pack.

"Done. I have the rest of the medical stuff and a bunch of hydropods and chips."

"You're a natural. Do you have any thermal camping gear by chance? I know we only planned for a half a day—"

Heat flooded my neck and face. "Well, you know me. I still hoped we'd find a way to extend the excursion, so I may have brought a conduction tent and a couple of blankets."

"Perfect! You're literally a lifesaver. Now we need to exit the craft and get our bearings." He frowned at the doors, half buried in snow and facing downward.

"Why? Isn't it protecting us from the elements?" I asked, wide-eyed.

"Can't you feel the cold?" he asked, the question filled with worry as opposed to challenge. He examined the beehive of airbags surrounding us.

"I do, but won't it be worse out there?" I asked as he located an area far brighter than the rest. When I squinted, I could see the broken shell behind the material.

Austin pressed his palms against the inflated material blocking the way. "Maybe, but when the sun goes down, even the temperature inside will be too harsh. But if we can find some kind of natural shelter that's big enough to set up the tent you brought..."

That was a nice way of saying we'd freeze to death anyway if we stayed here.

I swallowed, taking in the information. "Can you tear it?"

"This stuff is made tough. I can't break it with brute force," he said thoughtfully.

"Right. Okay."

Austin slid over to his bag and unzipped the part he could reach. He rummaged inside and came out with a bendable tube the size of a metal drinking straw.

"A laser cutter!" I said, understanding.

Austin held the tip to the closest airbag and squeezed. A bright blue light sliced at the stubborn material, popping it like a balloon. Slowly, he guided it in a large arc, clearing enough space for us to get through.

The full force of the arctic temperature burst inside along with sunlight, gusts of snow and wind, and a way forward. He was right. We could do this. The rest would be easy compared to crashing.

But my celebration was interrupted by Austin stumbling backward and grabbing his head. Rushing to his side, I held him steady until he was able to focus on me. He reached down and stroked my cheek with his thumb.

"It's probably just a concussion. I've had them before, plenty of times," he said.

I knew from experience he was a good liar, but in this case, I appreciated it. So I tucked myself beneath his arm and helped guide him out of the hellipod.

Our protective clothing helped, but it wouldn't keep us warm enough forever. The important thing was walking away alive, I reminded myself as we stumbled from the crash site. When he pointed to some large rocks covered in snow, I set him down there and caught my breath.

From this distance, the pod resembled a crushed tin can, discarded and half buried. I grimaced, knowing it wouldn't be much help in getting us back to the resort, but maybe some of it could be helpful.

"Where are you going?" Austin called as I trudged back toward the craft.

I held up a finger to let him know to wait and made my way to the where the bottom of the hellipod stuck half-out of the snow. I found two of the large hover disks that served as its landing legs, which were well above ground and not bent. So I grappled for a unitool in my bag and unscrewed them, finally prying them each free with a foot against the bottom of the craft for leverage.

When I returned, Austin was smiling at me—the goofy, genuine kind of smile I liked so much.

"How do I check you for brain damage?" I asked, hugging myself and dancing more from nerves than the need to keep warm.

"That was good thinking. But you haven't even noticed where we are yet," he said. "At least I got you to the spot you wanted."

I stilled, looking around. We'd crashed on the opposite side of the cave-like area next to the fjord. It was within around twenty meters of where the dogs had freaked out the day before.

"You don't look happy," Austin pointed out, furrowing his brow. "I thought you wanted to check this place out. You said you saw movement."

"I saw more than movement yesterday." I explained the ordeal with the dogs as Austin listened carefully.

When I finished, he stood, stumbling only slightly with a flinch. He turned to search the rocks and the overhang they created, though from this vantage point it wasn't as easy to see inside.

Rummaging in my bag, I came up with my binoculars and handed them to Austin. He popped them on his face and limped toward the rocks.

"Wait! Where are you going? What if there's a monster in there?" I rushed to catch up to him, which took a pathetic amount of time considering I was relatively uninjured.

"It's our best chance for shelter. If we check it out now, we have the advantage of daylight, which is good considering how short it is this time of year. It could be worse. We could be here during the part of the year where it's night almost twenty-four hours a day." He waited for me to catch up.

"Shouldn't we at least have a weapon of some sort?" I reasoned, trying to ignore the way my stomach knotted with the memory of the dogs' reaction.

Austin held up the laser cutter with a shrug and marched onward.

I couldn't believe that my opinion of him had changed so thoroughly in the last hour. My head spun from the accident and his about-face. But he'd wrapped around me like old-fashioned bubble wrap in that pod, risking everything without a second thought. And that kiss...damn that kiss was so raw. There was no faking that.

One thing was for sure. When we did get set up, we needed to talk. First thing was first, though. We had to search the area for animals and possibly worse.

I didn't like the idea of being unarmed after the way the dogs behaved yesterday, but I also knew Austin was hurt, and we weren't in a position to fuck around. I wanted to believe that Austin Cooper, who'd survived some of the most dangerous situations nature could conjure, would be able to handle anything. But he'd already admitted to never running into a cryptid. Could he take on a monster? Could I?

On the upside, the pod hadn't exploded like in the movies.

Walking over the ice and snow, even in specially designed boots, took double the effort of a simple hike. Add to that the layers of clothing and my supplies, and I found myself fatigued by the time we reached the edge of the rocks.

Wind kicked up, peppering my face with flecks of sharp ice that had me hiding in the crook of my elbow. Then Austin was there again, shielding me with his back. I felt him before I looked up. He was like the sun and a shield between his body heat and shelter.

"That came out of nowhere!" I yelled over what sounded like a pack of wolves howling in pain but was only the wind. I hoped.

Austin grimaced beneath his mask and took my arm to guide me forward. I copied his movements, shielding with my free arm and focusing on my footing. We walked at an angle to the wind so we weren't fighting it directly, and after what felt like an hour, we made it the last few meters to the overhang. Between the exertion and the terror of what we might find, my heartbeat kicked up into heart attack territory when I approached the unseen area.

Guiding me wordlessly around the chunks of ice and rock that surrounded the flattened boulders, Austin rounded the bend with me in tow. What I'd thought from afar to be a cave was in reality more of a large formation of boulders, ice, and snow with a long, flat, angled slab of stone that acted like a roof. The moment we made it underneath, I collapsed on my ass, out of breath, exhausted, and finally away from the wind and sideways blizzard that had infiltrated the air like a swarm of bees.

"Fuck," I said, slipping my pack off my shoulders, relieved to find the space devoid of other lifeforms.

But when I glanced at Austin, he'd already made his way to the back corner and was carefully pressing on the rocks before beckoning me over.

"Rosi! I found an entrance that looks like it angles downward."

Yanking the bag with me, I made my way to his side and saw an opening in the wall, hidden behind a crag but big enough for both of us if we wriggled in sideways and Austin ducked.

"What's in there?" I asked, not getting the best vibe from the complete darkness.

Austin tilted his head, considering. "Possibly better shelter. Possibly an animal's home. Do you have a lantern?"

I felt in my bag and pulled out the hand-sized sphere, pressing the sides to turn on the soft glow of white light. "You lead the way," I told him, not even pretending to be brave.

Austin nodded and took the lantern, reaching through the opening first. I followed behind him as closely as possible.

Once we cleared the entrance, the space opened up enough to move forward comfortably, and I clutched Austin's shoulder as he led the way down a twisted path. When he stopped with a gasp, my heart raced, but he held up the light to reveal a series of three path-ways leading into caverns in different directions.

"Which way?" I whispered, feeling strange about disturbing the still air.

Austin pointed the light to the right, and it fell on the unmistak-able arrangement of stones that made an *inuksuk* marker like I'd seen in the museum. Someone had been here.

"I thought no one lived in this area because of the elements," I said.

"If someone is here, it would explain what you saw. And if they have supplies, we'll be set for the night. Besides, I'd rather deal with another human than a monster if I have a choice."

"Okay," I said, taking a deep breath. It was true it didn't seem likely an animal had placed the marker, but no one really knew how intelligent cryptids were. I chose to keep my concerns to myself as it wouldn't be helpful to voice my worries.

Austin continued down the path marked by the *inuksuk,* and as we rounded a curve, the end came into view. It was a circular area of smooth stone, about twice the size around as the hellipod and four times as high. The front of the archway was covered in plastic sheeting to protect from the elements, but the whole side had been ripped into three long strips like something had clawed it from top to bottom.

Inside were two stacks, one as high as my shoulders and filled with random objects—everything from plates and cups to back-packs and clothing. Austin moved toward the second pile that was half as high but a million times as worrisome.

"Is that—" I said, hand shaking as I lifted it to point toward the small mountain.

"Bones," Austin confirmed, meeting my eyes with pure panic.

The globe in his hand went out and plunged us into pure blackness.

20

ROSI

"DON'T PANIC," AUSTIN SAID THROUGH THE DARK. THEN THE BLUE laser cut through the air toward the ground as he made his way back toward me. "Do you have anything else?"

Trying to breathe, I rummaged through my pack until I found the lighter I'd brought in case we needed to start a fire. I flicked it on, and Austin flipped off the laser.

"We need to get out of here," I said, trying so hard to do what he instructed and not panic.

"What do you think this is?" Austin asked, shaking the ball in his hands and smacking it until it blinked to life once again, throwing a very human skull on the ground into clear relief.

I swallowed back the bile rising in the back of my throat as I locked gazes with the black holes of the eye sockets. What appeared to be teeth marks engraved the forehead like twisted tattoos. "It looks like a nest."

Thankfully, Austin did not ask what would make a nest of bones and objects. Because none of the possibilities that came to mind were pleasant. Instead, he began rifling through the top of the pile of objects.

"What are you doing?" My voice cracked with panic as he froze with a tin can in hand.

"I'm looking for weapons or materials to make a fire."

I shook my head. "Fire could attract it, and the tent has conduction tech, so it'll warm itself with our body heat. And as for weapons, it didn't do them much good." I nodded at the skull on the ground. "We should get out of here."

"Come on." Austin grabbed my hand without protest, and we backtracked to the *inuksuk* and went to the path on the opposite side.

I tugged him to a halt. "Shouldn't we be getting out of the caverns altogether?"

Austin cupped my face, and his expression said he wasn't as certain as he'd seemed before. "It's still our best chance at avoiding freezing solid. If we can make it through the night, then we can hike back to the resort in the morning. Maybe whatever did that is no longer nearby."

I frowned. "You don't actually believe that do you?"

"Fine," Austin admitted, shifting his weight. "But if we're not near its nest, then maybe it will never know we were here."

Hesitating, I wanted to argue that I'd rather freeze than be added to a pile of bones. But he was right. It was logical, and we didn't have much choice. If we camped up there at the entrance it would see us for sure if it came back tonight. If we did it this way, there was a chance it would never realize we were there. Camping outside of the sheltered area was too big of risk because of the elements, and that limited our choices drastically.

Slipping off my pack, I pulled a small bag from the front pocket. Then I shoved the rest at him. "Go set up the tent. It'll add an extra layer of protection since we don't know how far the temperature will drop down here. I'll be there in a few minutes."

"What are you doing?" he asked, handing me the lantern and taking the lighter from me.

I paused, kneeling by the front of the passageway. "I'm throwing off the scent if that's what it uses."

Austin grinned and took off down the passage while I opened the bag and scattered the chips of pine around the entrance. They were covered in a special blend of aromas, a useful addition to a cryptid hunter's backpack.

By the time I'd caught up, Austin had the tent assembled in a corner across from a pool that cast a florescent, blue glow. Looking closer, I realized the glow came from stones beneath the surface of the water. The pool appeared to have formed over time, having collected slowly from the drippings off the wall and the stalactites above. If I wasn't so unnerved by the whole experience, I'd have called it romantic.

He waited at the front of the tent with the entrance open. I crawled inside with him following behind. Austin pulled the pack in with us and zipped up the seal.

"Talk to me," I said as I copied Austin, pulling off my parka and bunching it into a pillow. Now that we were inside the thermal protection of the tent, the temperature was only slightly chilly and would warm with our body temperatures soon. But the cold was the least of my worries at the moment. Out there, beyond the thin layer of carbon fiber laced material, was the monster of my nightmares.

"I'm so sorry, Rosi," Austin said, watching me with his knees to his chest. His entire body trembled, and I remembered his head injury. What if he'd hidden more from me?

"For what? This isn't your fault," I said, sitting across from him and rubbing my arms to prevent my hands from shaking.

"What if it is?" he asked, taking one of my hands and setting his on top between us.

"It isn't," I said, sliding farther in and still desperate to wipe visions of bones and teeth from my mind. "Take off your clothes so I can see if you have any other injuries. I'll get the med supplies out."

He acquiesced without any snide remarks and freed himself of his shirt, turning so his back was before me.

My hands flew to cover my mouth and prevent the gasp that threatened to break loose. Large, purple bruises bloomed across his skin. One disappeared into the waistband of his pants.

"You may have to take off your pants too," I said, reaching for another RR injection for lack of other options. That had to hurt like hell.

"Whether I want to admit it or not, Jackson was right," Austin said through a hiss as I pressed the meds into him. "All of the tech issues happen when I'm around."

I grabbed an ointment that I'd scooped up with everything else while trying to be patient with him. "Correlation doesn't equal causation, Austin."

"There's more to it, Rosi. Nearby electronics go wonky when my emotions are out of control."

I smoothed the ointment gently onto the bottom bruise and tucked a stray curl behind my ear. I wanted to dismiss his theory, but wasn't that what people had always done to me? Maybe there was something to what he suggested. Stranger things had happened.

"Tell me more," I said instead, guiding him down onto his side over the emergency blankets he'd laid out and lying to face him. At the very least, this was a good distraction for both of us with who knew what out there somewhere. His expression melted into relief, demonstrating I'd made the right decision.

"You make a great doctor, Rosi," he said in his low, vibrating, panty-soaking voice. "And an amazing friend. That's why you deserve better than me."

Clearly, it was time to finish what we'd started discussing before the crash, because I didn't believe that for one second. I cupped his face, running my thumb over the coarse, blond stubble and waited for him to continue.

"Her name was Sara," he said, and my thumb stilled on his cheek.

I wasn't expecting that.

"Okay," I said, "keep going."

He smiled wistfully. "She was my sister."

Oh. My thumb resumed stroking. Did he say *was*, as in past tense?

"We used to compete in everything together. She beat my best times more often than not. She was better at just about everything. Five years ago, we went to Niagara Falls. We ziplined, we hiked, it was great. Until we decided to run the gorge in a kayak."

I swiped a stray tear from the corner of his eye as he took a breath.

"Sara wanted to steer. We argued, and as usual, she won. But when the current became too much, I fought her instincts and instead of following her lead, I tried to take over. I was sure I was right. Ultimately, we were both too stubborn to let the other take charge, even though I'd agreed ahead of time." He stopped to sob, his face straining with the weight of something he'd carried for far too long.

I stroked his head and held him at the crook of my neck while he shook. When he quieted, I pulled away and studied him, my heart breaking for him. I knew enough to understand that two people trying to steer a tandem kayak was bad news. They were experts, but they'd let their sibling rivalry get in the way of common sense.

"It was my hubris that killed her, Rosi. She died because I couldn't control my emotions. I couldn't ignore my own instincts even when it made things worse."

I shook my head. "Austin, it was a horrible accident. She could have stopped and listened or let you take over too. It isn't all on you."

He smiled like he didn't believe me but appreciated the words. "I knew after that I had to do something so I'd never endanger another life, never hurt another human being. I traveled the world, putting myself at risk with crazier and crazier challenges because the adrenaline helped me escape the reality of a normal world without Sara. That's when I climbed Everest and met the Tibetan monks. They taught me how to calm my mind, and I've been practicing ever since."

So that was why I saw him stop and take deep breaths so often. It made sense and wasn't the worst outcome, considering. But...

"You suppress your emotions because you're afraid of them." It was a statement, not a question.

Austin searched my eyes, his darting back and forth as he looked for something. "I'm dangerous, Rosi. Dangerous to you if you get too close. That's why I did what I did at the news conference. It was stupid and cowardly, and I am so sorry."

"You pushed me away because you were scared you'd hurt me."

His lids lowered so that his lashes kissed his cheeks. He nodded.

I flicked him on the arm. It wasn't hard enough to hurt his head injury, but it probably smarted enough to get my point across.

"Ow!" His eyes snapped open as he reached for the spot.

"Last time I say this, Austin. You don't get to make decisions for me."

He nodded, eyes wide before a slow smile spread over his face.

"What?" I bristled at his reaction.

"You are fucking hot when you're angry."

The heat that rushed through me had nothing to do with the thermal tent or blanket. But he wasn't distracting me now that he'd made a breakthrough. "So how does all this equal you causing tech issues?" I pressed.

"I don't know, but I have a theory. I was so good at quieting my emotions that when they started to surface again, the intense energy messed with the tech."

"Hmm." My mounting anxiety longed for release, and my body knew exactly what release it wanted. I ran a finger over his lower lip. This close to him, I longed to suck it in my mouth.

I shook myself. "It's a reasonable theory, but we need more evidence. What brought your emotions back to the surface if you became so good at suppressing them?"

"I don't like that word," he said.

"Suppress? It's what you're doing. And meditation or not, it isn't healthy. Calm is good in tough situations, but feeling is what makes us human, Austin. You can't make yourself a machine so that you don't hurt."

"Good or bad, you're the one that brings my emotions to the surface. I don't know if it's timing or chemistry or fate, but you get right in my soul, Rosi, right through all my barriers."

I couldn't help but smile at that. It was the best compliment I'd ever had. And the truth was, he got to me just as much.

"I am still angry about you doing that ridiculous news conference. But it did make me realize something about myself too. I've been looking for validation from others when their opinions shouldn't matter. From now on, I trust myself, and if you don't like it, you can bite me."

"Can I bite you if I do like it?" Austin asked, nipping at my finger and making me laugh.

"Behave and I might forgive you for past choices, so long as you promise to talk to me in the future."

"I'll do whatever you want. But, Rosi, I mean it. I'm dangerous to be around. I take risks for a living."

"Oh, and being with someone who hunts monsters that keep nests full of the bones of their victims isn't a risk?" I asked, squeezing his face in my hand. "Seriously though, Austin. Please don't push me away. I'll make that decision for myself."

Reaching for a tendril of my hair, he tucked it back behind my ear, which elicited shivers throughout my body. "I couldn't stay away from you if I wanted to. You have my word."

"Maybe you should stay away for *your* own good," I said before I could stop myself. "Since we're being all honest, I should probably tell you that I've been having nightmares that may or may not be premonitions."

Austin cupped my cheek and waited with so much patience for me to continue that he made it harder to talk instead of easier. But I pushed through. "It started before I came here, and each vision has been more detailed than the last. They all include a monster. Something I've never seen before, though I can't get a great look at it, at least that I remember."

"What does it do?"

"It chases us," I said and fought the urge to stuff a curl in my mouth.

Austin didn't flinch. "Us?"

I nodded. "You are running with me in the snow. We're headed toward the resort when it catches up." Tears fell as I recalled the blood and the horror that gripped me when I woke.

"I won't let it hurt you, Rosi."

"It isn't me that dies in the dream, Austin."

We lay silently for several minutes as Austin continued to cup my face and stare. Finally, he smiled sadly, wiping at a stray tear with his thumb. "I am on your side, just like I said. Besides, if it happens out in the snow, then we should be safer in here for tonight."

I moved back, pulling out of his grip as I leaned up on my elbows. "I appreciate you trying to make me feel better, but I don't want you to die for me, Austin."

"I'm not planning on it," he said, still far too calm. "Even if there's truth in the dream, that doesn't mean it has to happen exactly that way. Maybe it was a warning so we could do things differently."

The fact that he once again did not dismiss me or my experiences made my heart warm and swell. But it made the pain at the possibility of losing him that much sharper.

"What if—"

"Rosi, I've looked death in the face more than once and made it out alive. I will do anything for you."

"Will you do what I want or what you think you should?" I challenged, scooting closer again because it hurt to be too far from him.

"What you want—as long as you tell me what that is."

I relaxed. I had already said I didn't want him dying for me. But there were other things I wanted and needed from him. "Maybe I should test that out," I mused.

Austin grinned. "Try me."

I licked my lips and took stock of my feelings. I was bursting with extremes. On the one hand, I was frightened out of my wits by what real-life nightmare might be out there, and I was in shock from the crash. I craved a distraction. On the other, I was smitten by the man next to me and undeniably attracted to him. So smart or not, the solution I had in mind solved both issues in one way or another. Besides the meds should be working for him by now.

"Take off your clothes," I commanded.

Austin watched me as he slipped his pants off along with the dark-blue briefs I doubted that obnoxious news woman would ever have enough imagination to predict.

"Did you want to examine me for further bruises?" he asked.

"I don't remember asking you to talk," I said, placing a finger against his lips. He held up his hands in surrender.

"Good. Now help me take off my clothes. I believe I read somewhere that skin-to-skin contact helps keep people warm in these situations."

Austin rolled his eyes, letting me know how silly that was when we were protected by the tech of the tent. But he reached for my shirt and slowly lifted it, skimming my sides with his hands as he did so. Gooseflesh rose at his touch, and I nearly moaned because I'd missed it so much. I'd become addicted to Austin Cooper after one long, beautiful night. He was my drug of choice and possibly just as dangerous as the worst of them in the long term.

21

AUSTIN

HER BRA CLASPED IN THE FRONT. I SPLAYED A HAND ACROSS THE delicate skin of her chest as she stretched out beneath me. Without breaking eye contact, I released her breasts from their silken prison. Both her nipples and my cock were hard and ready. But this was going to be a long night, and I wanted it to be one she'd always remember.

I started to take one of her nubs in my mouth, but she shoved me back.

"Nuh-uh. I said undress."

Damn. Her commanding attitude turned me on more than her perfect curves.

"Yes, ma'am," I said, and yanked her pants down and off, smacking the side of the tent as I did so.

The panties she had on were not exactly practical, but fuck, I was glad she wore them. At the risk of more admonishment, I tugged them upward instead of off, pulling the thin strip of satin material against her most sensitive parts and watched her gasp, mouth parted. It almost undid me.

"Off," she whispered, and I complied.

"Now what do you want, Rosi?" I asked, crawling up over her so that my length slid across her leg, tauntingly close to her core.

She stared up at me with half-lidded eyes filled with lust. "So many options. What do you want to do?" she teased.

"I want to taste you. You're like the best dessert I've ever had, sweet like sugarcane."

"I'll permit it," she squeaked.

Laughing at her reaction, I slid back down, sampling bits of her along the way. Her nipples, the soft spot beneath her breasts, her stomach, her thighs...

By the time I licked her folds, they were soaked with her need, and I had to grab my own shaft as I nipped and sucked and slipped my tongue inside of her.

"So good," I said from between her legs. It was everything I'd been dreaming about since the news conference, everything I thought I'd thrown away for her own safety.

"Keep going," she said, guiding my head back down.

I let go of myself and slid two fingers inside her, covering her clit with my mouth. The slick heat around my digits made my cock jerk in anticipation, but I reached higher and began slipping them in and out in a fierce rhythm as I lavished attention on her most sensitive spot. Feeling her muscles clench around me, I knew she was close, so I slowed, giving one last, long lick to the spot I'd been focused on.

"Do you want me to continue, Rosi?" I asked.

"Fuck you," was her answer.

"Don't mind if I do, but first, you." I picked up the pace again, dipping my head down to suck her clit into my mouth, lightly scraping it with my teeth as she bucked and cried out with a beautiful groan. "Keep going?" I asked, almost breathless from the excitement it stirred in me.

Her reply this time was unintelligible. So I used my hands to bring her the rest of the way as I watched her face. I nearly came with her. I'd never seen anything so beautiful as Rosi falling over the precipice with my fingers inside her. But I wasn't a novice. Sex was another source of adrenaline, and despite having a year's break, I was far from celibate. So I continued my ministrations, and her orgasm persisted for as long as her body allowed.

When she finally collapsed, out of breath, I withdrew my fingers and sucked off the sweet taste of her.

"Thank you for letting me do that," I said, crawling up over her once again.

"You're welcome," she said through a heavy breath and smile that nearly blinded me.

I squeezed her breast and ran a finger over her nipple.

"Did I say you could do more?" She panted.

I paused with her nipple between my fingers and raised an eyebrow in question.

"Lie down," she said. "It's my turn. But, uh, we can change that if it hurts to be on your back."

My injuries no longer hurt thanks to the meds and her distractions, so I let myself grin as I lay back down for her.

22

ROSI

TAKING MY TIME, I WAS DETERMINED TO EXAMINE AND EXPLORE EVERY one of Austin's perfectly sculpted ridges. I traced the muscles of his shoulders down over his pectorals and back and forth over the dips in his abdominals. I followed with my mouth, doing whatever pleased me the most, including tugging on his nipple with my teeth. His sharp intake of breath let me know I made a good choice.

When I reached his cock, I took it in my hand, feeling the weight and girth of it as the muscles in my core tightened with hunger. I slid my grip over him and back again, watching as he shut his eyes and caught his lower lip with his teeth.

Lowering my head, I licked the bit of precum off the tip.

"Fuck, Rosi. I hope I last."

"You will because I'm still in charge and there's no coming until I do again." This whole dominatrix thing felt good.

I straddled him, sliding my slickness against him before taking him inside me all the way. Rocking back and forth, I slid my palms up his chest. His hands reached into the air on either side of me and stayed there, like it took all his control not to grab me.

"Okay." I panted. "Do what you want." Because I was pretty sure doing what he wanted was going to feel really damn good again.

He grasped my hips and began thrusting upward into me, holding me down to take the full impact of each push.

I screamed his name as he filled me over and over again.

"I can't hold it much longer," he barked.

"Me first," I said, knowing I was so close.

He slid a hand down between us and pressed a thumb against my clit, rubbing it in fast, sloppy circles as he continued to thrust.

The sounds I made no longer resembled names or words as the tension inside me exploded into a cascade of spasms of release. Austin grabbed my hips again and thrust up off the ground, knees bent as the orgasm ripped through him. He throbbed inside me as he called my name.

I collapsed onto him and rolled to the side where he held me close. The only sound for a long time was our breathing. Then, propping himself up on one elbow, Austin gazed down at me, drinking in my body in a way that made me flush and squirm.

"You are so beautiful, Rosi," he said, eyes returning to my lips.

"You're not half bad yourself, lover boy," I quipped, but it came out in a whisper.

He dipped his mouth to mine. This time our kiss was slow and languid, making the heat build inside me all over again until I felt starved for his body, starved for release.

Without disconnecting his exploration of my mouth, Austin positioned himself over me, and slid inside. His thrusts were slower this time, agonizingly so, but the passion he put into his every movement drove me closer and closer to the edge of bliss.

My hands were everywhere—his chest, his neck, his biceps which bulged as he held himself above me, and finally his ass as I tried to make him move faster. But instead, he went deep, angling his hips upward and driving into me completely.

I moaned, head tipping back away from his mouth. So he found my neck as he thrust again, building in momentum until he lifted me from the ground with each dive inside.

"Faster," I begged.

He complied, burying himself in me again and again until we both fell apart all over again.

"Your stamina is worthy of an award," I said. A sheen of sweat covered my body.

I could feel it when he said, "I'm not done with you yet."

When I opened my eyes, I was nestled against him, his arm over my hip, his hand on my ass. He was beautiful when he slept, like all the weight of the world was released from his shoulders. His scruff had grown, and he had a rough, golden beard that framed his square jaw. My hand slid over his heart, feeling the reassuring thump until his eyes fluttered open. He grinned, focusing on me, and it looked like sunlight pouring in an open window.

"Good morning," he said, voice husky with sleep.

"Morning," I said, giving him a soft peck on the lips. "It appears we made it through the night without being eaten alive."

"I thought I'd done a pretty good job at eating you last night."

I smacked his chest half-heartedly. "You know what I mean."

"Then let's get our things packed up and hike back to the resort while we have the sun on our side."

That sounded like the best idea I'd heard in ages. So we pulled on our clothes and packed everything inside the tent into my bag as fast as we could. When Austin reached to open the zippered door, I stuffed a chunk of hair in my mouth to prevent a gasp from escaping. Every muscle in my body tensed as the blast of cold rushed in to meet us.

Following Austin outside, I relaxed when nothing moved, aside from the slow drip of water sliding off a stalactite and disturbing the pool of water with a lazy ripple. Austin folded the tent quickly and expertly then stepped in front of me. He tugged my balaclava down over my face, leaving his hand on my cheek for a moment, his silvery eyes the only things showing of his own head like two beautiful crystals.

"Ready?" he asked, offering his hand.

Nodding, I clasped his gloved palm to mine, and we made our way back down the path toward the main cavern. I wondered if he could feel the way my heart thumped against my ribs. If I rested my head on his chest, would I hear his pumping hard with adrenaline too?

When we crossed the threshold to the point of the three offshoot tunnels, I relaxed, again seeing nothing waiting for us. The scent decoy must have helped. I made a mental note to add that to my private journal.

We'd made it all the way to the sloped exit path when the sound of stones sliding down rock made me pause.

Austin tensed, so I knew he'd heard it too. I looked at him, silently asking what we should do.

A low snarl echoed around the large chamber. We both slowly turned toward the three openings at the other end of the cave. A crash came from the path with the nest and made me cringe. After a moment of silence, several large rocks and a couple of bones came rolling from the opening.

"Should we run?" Austin whispered as the snuffs and growls of something grew closer.

Right. I was the expert on this. "If we run it might automatically chase us," I said, trying to think. "Start moving backward, up the path as slowly and quietly as you can."

My mouth was dry as Austin led the way behind me. I used my hands to keep balanced on either side of the narrow corridor as I glanced back and forth between my footing and the spot where I was sure something horrible would burst through at any moment. The dreams I'd had flashed in my mind, raising my pulse rate until the drumbeat in my head drowned out all other sound. *The teeth— the blood.*

The bite of cold air at the nape of my neck told me we were close to the exit. The path grew steeper, making me pay more attention to my precarious balance so as not to set loose too many stones and make too much noise. As we curved away from the sightline, the very air above the rocks and bones that had shot from the tunnel shifted. A warbling I associated with a mirage of heat above asphalt made me question if my vision was blurred from fear.

Then the rocks and bones moved, stirring up into a small funnel of wind. My feet slipped, causing a mini avalanche of pebbles to bounce downward. *Shit.*

The rocks and bones stopped swirling and hung in mid-air. A pair of yellow eyes stared at me above them. There was no body attached, and my brain scrambled to try to fill one in. I couldn't tell if the blurred space was a product of my eyes or some sort of camouflage, but the effect was a mixture of terror and confusion. Then the free-floating orbs made eye contact with me, and my blood ran cold.

"Run!" My voice came out raspy, but I knew Austin heard because he grabbed my arm and helped yank my frozen feet up the rest of the way.

We burst through the crevice and out past the entrance to the rocky cavern. The storm had stopped, but a fresh layer of snow coated everything, erasing our footsteps from the day before. The sun shone above, though the wind still bit at any exposed skin, no matter how tiny.

I didn't care. I pumped my legs as hard as I could, forcing myself across the frozen tundra and away from the cave. Maybe the creature wouldn't follow us into the light. Some cryptids hated light, according to my research.

Squeezing my hand, Austin pulled me along in his wake. His long legs could go faster than my short ones, and he was built for this sort of exertion. Pure adrenaline made me fight to keep up as the sounds of crunching snow and growls like no animal I'd ever heard nipped at our heels.

"It's too far!" I yelled as the imposing beauty of the Glacial Palace Resort came into view on the horizon, reflecting rainbows up into the sky around its uppermost dome.

"No it's not," Austin said, pulling harder. "Focus on the goal. Just keep going forward. Don't stop, and don't look back."

Look back? The urge to do exactly what he'd said not to claimed me. What did it look like in the sunlight? Was it still using camouflage? What cryptid was it? Abominable snowman? *Aklut?* *Amorat?* It didn't sound like a wolf per se, but then again, I didn't spend a lot of time with wolves either.

The hair on the back of my neck stood on end as some sort of electric force filled the air around us. My back arched, and I sensed that something was about to grab me. Certain it was right there, I glanced over my shoulder.

I screamed.

Austin swung toward me, and I felt his arms around my waist, but I couldn't stop screaming and I couldn't look away. It was impossible. The thing was right there, not five feet from us. Its decaying gray body stood out starkly against the white and blue backdrop of the world around it. It towered above us—at least seven to eight feet of lean sinew and muscle. Its yellow eyes held mine, and they felt human, though it looked anything but with its double-wide mouth filled with rows of needlelike teeth that dripped with something that was either saliva or venom. I didn't want to find out which.

"When I spin you around, I want you to run." Austin's warm breath coated my ear as he spoke. "Don't look back, and don't stop for any reason."

"No." I remembered my dream in vivid detail. It was coming true, and I wasn't going to let Austin die. I wasn't. He promised me.

"Rosie, now is not the time to fight." Austin yanked me off my feet, and the next thing I registered was flying through the air. We'd be discussing this later.

I hit the ground hard and rolled like a log for several feet. By the time I righted myself, the snarls had turned to ear-piercing howls. Standing, I snatched my backpack from where it'd landed in the snow and dug inside.

Glancing over, I saw Austin tuck and roll away from a swipe of the thing's elongated arms. Its nails appeared as sharp and lengthy as its teeth. It made eye contact with me again as Austin readied himself for another attack. I swear it smiled then, the light in its eyes taunting me. I froze when I heard a scratchy masculine voice in my head.

It's always more fun when someone watches.

Then it leaned down on all fours and sprung at me.

I reached in my bag blindly, digging for anything that might help while a chunk of ice the size of a basketball hit the monster's legs. It howled again as it fell sideways, skidding a few feet before turning on Austin, who held another large piece of ice in his hands.

"Damn it, Rosi! Run!" Austin yelled, lobbing his weapon at the beast before prying another from the ground.

"I'm not leaving you," I said and pulled out a handful of what felt like pebbles from my pack.

A glance told me they were small crystals that Cora must've left in my bag as protection. Obviously, they didn't work. I scanned the collection of clear orange, and spotted, black stones. I dug again and found something bigger to yank loose.

This stone was pure black, so deep that it was hard to make out the ridges in the natural texture. Not tumbled was good, that left plenty of sharp points along the top. Maybe I could use it as a weapon.

I ran toward the creature, who'd re-focused on Austin. With each clump he pulled from the ground, the creature got closer.

I wasn't going to make it.

It made eye contact with me again just before it lunged, toppling Austin to the ground. It raised a claw, and I screamed as it swiped at him.

Throwing up an arm to protect himself, Austin tried to deflect its strike. But crimson spurted out through his parka. Austin cried out from the pain. The beast grabbed his injured arm, squeezing until the sound of snapping bones carried above the wind. The whole time its saffron eyes held mine, I saw pure pleasure in them.

Austin's head fell back, lolling to the side. He'd fainted from the pain. But the monster didn't care. It wanted my reaction, eyes locked on me as it opened massive jaws and lifted his bloody arm.

I ran toward them, clutching my weapon and screaming an angry war cry as its long, serpentine tongue swept Austin's blood from his arm, making a show of swallowing.

So good. Almost as good as a young one. I realized it was talking in my head and fought the urge to vomit.

But playing with me had allowed me enough time to reach them. The monster's smile melted into a look of anger as I launched my fist, which I was pretty sure was full of obsidian.

The howl that burst from its mouth brought me to my knees at Austin's side. I had barely grazed the thing, but its gilded stare was focused on the stone protruding from my fist. My heart beat faster as I considered the possibility that whatever horrible beast attacked us didn't like the type of crystal Cora had given me.

Cora, I love you. I held the stone out in front of me like it could fire lasers at the cryptid, and it might as well have because the closer I moved, the farther away it scurried and the more it hissed.

"I have more," I threatened. "Get back in your hole."

I will taste you, girl. It glared at me then ran on all fours back toward the rocks. The air around it shimmered, and the vision of the monster itself disappeared from view, confirming my suspicions about a camouflage ability. Still clutching the stone, I collapsed on my ass beside Austin .

One look brought back all of my nightmares. His arm, shoulder to fingers, was bathed in blood, skin turning blue and bones sticking out in places. He was a mangled mess, and the parka and thermal that had protected him was nothing more than shredded bits of cloth blowing in the breeze.

Scrambling into action, I lugged over my backpack. I didn't have much to make a splint out of, but I attempted to wrap Austin's mangled arm to his side with a bandage then pulled out the two hover disks I'd pried from the hellipod. I managed to get Austin on, so his head and shoulders rested on one and his pelvis balanced on the other.

"Hang in there," I said, wrapping one of the thermal blankets we'd used the night before around his wounded side.

Thankfully, the boards worked, and when I activated them, they lifted him above the ground. I steered him awkwardly in the direction of the resort, which still felt too far away, but I was determined. Once I got the hang of moving both boards at once with him on them, things moved faster.

The sun had begun to set by the time we reached the hill closest to the building. But Austin was so pale, and I was exhausted to the point of trembling with each step. So close and yet so far away. I wasn't giving up. I couldn't.

I paused to down another hydropod, though the contents were mostly frozen, and then forced us forward. The icy air had begun to seep inside my thermals, and I knew it had to be worse for Austin. My vision blurred as I shook beyond control.

At first I thought the barking was the beast coming back for us, but then I saw actual dogs cresting the hill, Yuka in the lead and almost blending in with the white background.

"Toklo?" I asked, my voice quivering as hard as the rest of me.

He pulled up beside me, taking in the sight of us, mouth hanging open. I knew Austin was in rough shape, but I had no idea how I looked.

"Need a ride?" he asked, already steering the disks onto the sled. "Yuka spotted you and wouldn't stop barking until I looked. How'd you get out there?"

I couldn't answer, and he didn't push me, probably well aware that hypothermia might be setting in. He threw some blankets over me as I settled down beside Austin on the sled. And as he turned the sled around, whisking us back to the safety and warmth of the resort, I could have sworn I heard a snarling sound coming from the bottom of the hill.

23

AUSTIN

I sat up with a start, and despite the panic and confusion gripping me, I knew from the full body ache I'd made a mistake. As my surroundings came into focus, my pulse settled, but only a bit. It was something like going from trapped-in-a-burning-building speed to something's-hiding-in-the-dark speed, a subtle but significant difference.

The last thing I remembered was that thing sinking its claws in and shredding my arm. A glance at my body revealed said arm was in a regenerative tank—sort of an aquarium-like casing filled with teal goo that stimulated tissue regeneration. The cooling sensation wasn't unpleasant and was far more welcome than the pain etched into my memory.

I'd made it to the medcenter. But where was Rosi? Had she run like I'd told her to? I hoped she had, but I worried it wasn't in her programming to take orders. The vision of that monster's teeth clamping over her made me shudder, and I had to start my breathing exercises to banish the thought from my mind.

"Hello?" I called.

Moments later, the doors swished open to reveal a woman with auburn hair and blue scrubs whom I recognized as the resort doctor. Her frown let me know she wasn't happy with me, but I didn't care.

"We've been here less than two weeks, and you've seen me twice, Mr. Cooper," she said, flicking at the holopad in her hand. "I know what you do for a living, but let's try to take a break while on vacation, yes?"

I cleared my throat. "Where's Rosi? Is she okay?"

The doctor's lips tipped up in a flicker of a smile before settling back into disappointment mode again. "Ms. Sanchez is fine. Her injuries were far less serious. You have her and Mr. Kootoo to thank for getting you back alive."

I relaxed back onto the hovercot and closed my eyes with relief. Of course she saved my life. I smiled and shook my head without looking as the doctor moved around, fiddling with electronics.

"She didn't want to leave, you know. Ms. Sanchez, I mean."

The doctor's words made me open my eyes again.

"Miss Bennet wanted to speak to you first. I've alerted her you are awake, and she should arrive soon."

My vision wavered, and I clenched my good fist as anger coursed through me. Nicole was my boss, not my mother. But as I opened my mouth to demand to see Rosi instead, the doors swished once again and she entered along with Nicole and Jackson.

Rosi tackled me, causing the bed to bob.

"Ow."

"I'm sorry!" She lifted her head but kept hold of my waist and good shoulder. "I'm so glad you're awake."

I grinned, wanting to smooth her hair from her face but realized I couldn't move my arm inside the tank. So I leaned up and planted a quick peck on her forehead.

"We're glad you're all right as well," Nicole said, stepping to the foot of the cot. "It seems we owe you an apology, Mr. Cooper. The electrical issues we experienced may have been your fault, but they were not under your control."

So my theory about my emotions was correct? It had to be if

Nicole and company were willing to believe something outside of their scientific reality. I really screwed up.

"It's not what you think," Rosi said, smoothing my hair like I'd wanted to do to hers.

Jackson nodded to the doctor who lifted a silver tray into view. On it was what looked like a chip one might find in a computer or holopad.

"What's that?" I furrowed my brow, staring at the tiny object.

"It's what was messing with the tech," Nicole said. "It was implanted in your shoulder and worked with the electrical signals from your amygdala."

"What?" I sat up again, forcing Rosi to back up. I looked from one face to another, waiting for them to bust out laughing like it was a bad joke. But they didn't.

"It was implanted there, and when I examined your injured arm, I found it." The doctor set down the tray. "The signal was weak from damage but still working. That's why it's in a dampening field."

A closer examination at the tiny chip revealed an even tinier magnet on the edge that apparently stopped it from transmitting.

"We traced the source, and thanks to you, we have a general idea where the would-be saboteur is hiding," Jackson said.

Nicole nodded. "It was likely implanted at your pre-flight physical. Which means we have a mole in our medical department at Bennet Systems. It's being dealt with as we speak."

Swallowing, I tried to wrap my head around what they'd said. "But how did I trigger it?"

"The amygdala is the part of the brain that controls emotions, Austin," Rosi said, sitting at my side, more gently this time.

Jackson continued, "When you had a strong emotional response, that triggered the chip to send out an electromagnetic pulse that disrupted tech around you."

I'd been used by someone as a weapon. My head pounded with

pain and too many competing thoughts. Good thing it wasn't in me anymore, or the whole place might've blown up.

"Wait," I said, snapping up straight yet again. "The monster—"

"We've recovered some video from the cameras we had on your parkas," Nicole said with a heavy sigh. "I'm not one to buy into monsters and fairytales, but it appears whatever animal found you, it wasn't a pleasant one."

"That wasn't an animal," Rosi said. "It was humanoid. There was intelligence in its eyes."

Nicole frowned and shifted her weight, swinging her long blond hair over her shoulder. "Well, whatever it is, it's a new species of something, and it didn't look human to me. But the short of it is, we are suspending all external activities until our probes find it and we can determine the best course of action, ecologically speaking."

Rosi squeezed my hand. "This is my area of expertise. I hate to say I wished for this, but I have been searching for proof of supposedly 'mythological' cryptids. If you need help figuring it out, let me know."

Nicole smiled, gave one sharp nod, and motioned for Jackson to follow her out of the room. She hesitated at the door, glancing back at me.

"Again, I do apologize, Austin. Please rest assured your ticket to the asteroid hike is already reserved."

"Asteroid hike?" Rosi asked as the doors closed and the doctor fiddled with the touchpad on the other side of the tank.

"It's why I took this job," I admitted, worried Rosi would see this as a permanent separation. And being permanently separated from her was unthinkable at this moment. "It's been a goal of mine to be one of the first to join in the space games."

"Sounds fun," she said, tilting her head in a flirty way as she leaned down to whisper in my ear. "If you get to bring a friend, I'd love to find out what zero-G sex is like."

Fuck, the suggestion alone made me start to harden beneath the thin blanket. I really wanted the doctor to leave. But I wasn't sure if I was allowed strenuous physical activity while my arm regenerated.

"When do I get out of here, doc?" I asked.

"One more day to be safe, Mr. Cooper, though I'm impressed with your body's healing capabilities."

Rosi climbed in the cot and settled in on my uninjured side, resting her head on my chest. I inhaled her vanilla bean scent.

"I don't know if the race would disturb your studies," I said, thinking seriously about her suggestion, "but if not, I'd love for you to come along."

She snuggled against me, stirring more thoughts of what I'd like to do and making me shift as well.

"I don't know if I'm going to continue the program, to be honest," she said.

"What? Why?"

She lifted her head and turned to face me. "I don't need to prove anything to anyone from here on out. I just don't know what my life's goal is if it isn't hunting cryptids."

"I don't know, but I'd be happy to be there while you figure it out," I said, staring into her eyes. Chocolate fondue was what they reminded me of, and that made me want to spend an evening eating the melted goodness off her body.

Rosi giggled, bringing her thigh to press against my erection. She winked. "I should let you recover. How about the second you're free, we catch up?"

"Wait for me in my room?" I asked. "Let Cora have yours."

Biting her lip, she nodded, and I was sure my flagpole would be noticeable to the doc. But whether out of professionalism or distraction, she said nothing.

The rest of the day bored me out of my mind. I was used to exercise. I tried to meditate, but even that eluded me because of my position. Or possibly because I kept thinking about Rosi in the cave, Rosi in space, and Rosi covered in chocolate fondu. I knew what we were having for dinner at least.

It was six hours after Rosi had left when I'd had enough. My arm inside the tank itched like crazy, and I was sure I'd been overcooked.

"Doc!" I called.

She'd sent in a nurse the last three times I'd asked her to help me get to the bathroom and hand me a fresh hydropod. But this time I waited, only to be greeted by silence.

"Doc?" I called again.

A crash and shuffling came from beyond the doors. I tensed. A familiar snarl followed, throwing my heart into overdrive.

I pushed the release on the tank and held my breath as the liquid inside drained out. The top popped open, and I finally pulled my arm free, wiggling my intact fingers. There was no time to marvel at the smooth flesh that should've been a mess of scars and grafts. I'd been lucky, and I knew it. All I had now was a sore shoulder. That I could deal with. I'd had worse.

It'd taken less than a minute to free myself, and I'd heard only silence since.

"Doc?' I called again, standing and searching for my clothes. I spotted a shirt and jeans in the corner and would have smiled if I weren't on such high alert. Rosi must have thought ahead and left them for me. I snatched the microchip still on the silver tray on impulse and shoved it in the pocket of the still folded pants. Glancing around for something I could use as a weapon, I came up empty but assured myself the growl was probably nothing more than PTSD hallucination from my attack in the tundra.

I was still snapping my jeans when I rushed out the door and stopped dead. Streaks of shining red splattered in droplets, like someone popped a water balloon in the middle of the office. Only this wasn't water in the balloon. I was pretty sure the shining scarlet painting the walls, desk, and doors was blood.

The sounds I'd heard weren't in my head. They'd been real, and I was too late to try and help.

Breathing deeply, I inched forward to peer behind the desk

where the chair was pulled away like the doc had stood up to greet someone. Or something.

I hadn't even heard a scream, that was how fast it must have happened. Was the doctor still alive somewhere? Judging by the amount of splatter, I doubted it. My stomach turned as I spotted what looked like a finger in the corner beside the desk. I gagged and nearly vomited but held it together as I lifted my wristcom.

"Nicole Bennet," I said. "Emergency. Nicole!"

"I'm here, Austin. What's happening?"

"I think the doctor is dead."

Silence for a moment, then, "Why?"

"There's a lot of blood, too much for one person to lose and be okay. And I heard it—the snarling and scratching."

"What did you hear, Austin?" Nicole demanded.

I swallowed back the bile that still fought to come up. "The thing that attacked me. It's inside the resort."

24

AUSTIN

My mind raced as I stood frozen in place. I was afraid if I moved, I'd step on the doctor's blood. To me that was tantamount to defacing her body. But I knew I should do something. I should find Rosi—get us to safety. Where or how, I had no idea. But the thought of walking in my room to find—

Stop it, Austin. The monks taught me to stop thoughts like these when I could. All such things did was panic me when I needed to stay in the present and deal with what was happening in the now. It was so easy when I was climbing or parasailing, but when it came to this, to Rosi, it was somehow different.

Wincing, I drew a deep breath. It was different because it involved someone I cared about. It wasn't just me on the line this time. Hell, it wasn't just us, it was the whole damn resort, and we'd led that thing here. I ignored the small voice that said it probably would've found us anyway at some point.

When leaping off a cliff, it was important not to hesitate. So I moved, eyes focused on the door. When I made it outside, it was as if the entire world had been frozen and then exploded to life. Jackson marched down the hall with a handful of others in his wake. His pale face probably looked normal compared to mine. He hadn't even seen the devastation yet.

Nicole's voice filled the halls through the comm system, too loud despite her calm tone.

"Due to potential unforeseen issues with our climate control system, we are disappointed to announce that we are evacuating the resort and cutting the vacation short. Please proceed to boarding immediately. We will have AI staff pack and send on your belongings as they will not be affected by the temperature drop."

Flashing blue lights bathed the halls as the cleanup team rushed past me into the medcenter. Jackson paused in front of me as Nicole's voice continued over the sounds of nervous chatter and footsteps rushing down the halls toward the evacuation.

"We at Bennet Systems hope you've had an exceptional stay here at the Glacial Palace and look forward to serving you again when all the inevitable bugs with such new technology are worked out. We apologize for the inconvenience and would like to offer a short stay at the Time Capsule Resort as compensation."

Jackson squeezed my arm. "Get to the plane, Austin. Thank you for your help." He turned to go.

"I'm not getting on a plane until I find Rosi," I said, stopping him in his tracks.

"I'm sure she heard the announcement and is headed that way too," Jackson said. His tone might've been reasonable, but his voice raised a whole octave.

"Don't tell me Nicole isn't calling her in to confer with as we speak," I said, knowing in my bones the truth of the statement. "She offered earlier, and Nicole wants this taken care of as quickly and quietly as possible, so I know she'll ask her."

Jackson swallowed and released my arm. "It's her choice. If she's scared, no one will stop her from leaving."

I smiled as Nicole's message played on repeat. "I'm not worried about you forcing her. I *know* her. Rosi's not walking away—she's going to try to figure it out. And if she is, then I am too."

Staring at me for a moment, Jackson finally relented, relaxing his shoulders. "Nicole won't like having the risk of collateral damage, but she'll get it. She'll probably even appreciate it."

A crowd of teenagers rushed past us, forcing us closer to the door of the Medcenter. Jackson pressed something into my hand.

"What's this?" I asked, frowning down at the small, three-pronged object.

"It's a weapon. It works like a stun gun without any physical contact. If you're staying here, you need to be able to defend yourself."

I nodded, turning it in my hand. It seemed simple enough with a single button to depress and a safety release where my thumb would go if I held it toward someone. "What about you?" I asked.

"I've got another weapon and a whole team of people. Don't worry about me. Nicole and Rosi should be up on the sixth floor."

"Thank you," I said and swam upstream into the tide of people headed my way.

When I got to the tubes, they were all filled with people coming down to the ground floor. I could have waited for one to empty and ridden it back up for the next crowd, but even if I were patient enough for that, there was no guarantee it would be going to floor six.

So I did what I knew how to do. I hoisted myself onto the edge of the glass tank at the base of the waterfall and balance-walked my way to the rocks, where I switched into climbing mode. My newly healed shoulder twinged as I hoisted myself up onto the first boulder, but with a few stretches, the tightness melted and the pain dulled to a background thrum no worse than any other injury I'd endured in my travels.

But as I leaped to reach for the top of the next stone step, my fingertips grazed the ice and I slipped, narrowly catching myself before I toppled to the ground.

I pulled myself up to the next step and froze. That was a rooky mistake, and not one that I could afford to make, ever. Sure, things had happened that were out of my control before, but I'd never been so off-balance while climbing.

Heart pounding in my ears, I swallowed hard. I didn't have time for this. Rosi was in danger, and I had to get to her. But what good would I be if I suddenly lost my mojo? Visions of the medcenter swam in my head, and I covered my mouth to prevent retching.

Pressing my hands to my knees, I forced myself to breathe, counting carefully in my mind. There was so much blood...

What if I could have done something? It was like Sara all over again. What if I was more of a hinderance than a help to Rosi? To everyone?

Breathe, Austin, I told myself. *You let Sara down, but there was nothing you could have done for the doc. It happened too fast.*

I nodded and glanced up at the wall of boulders still before me. The tubes to my left were still filled with people being evacuated.

It should have taken all of ten minutes to scale the entire thing, but in that moment, it felt like an impossibility. If I bailed now, I wouldn't be a liability to Rosi. Maybe that was the way to protect her.

"Please don't push me away," she'd said in the cave. The memory made my heart lurch. How could I even think of abandoning her? I wasn't the same kid I'd been in the raft with Sara. I was a fucking adult who'd studied with Tibetan monks and traveled to the harshest places on the planet. This was my last fear, the fear of letting someone in and then letting them down, and I was going to conquer it like I had Kilimanjaro. *I'm coming, Rosi.*

I spread my legs hip-width apart and sank my weight into my feet. Then I eyeballed the ledge of the next step and leaped for it, planning my fingerholds in advance.

By the time I reached the sixth floor ten minutes later, I found Nicole, Rosi, and her friend Cora in the hall arguing.

The moment Rosi's eyes met mine, she launched herself at me, and I caught her around the waist as she threw her arms around my neck.

"Awww," Cora squeaked.

Rosi ignored her and buried her face in the crook of my neck. Moisture from her tears slid down my skin, and I gripped her tighter.

"I thought I wouldn't get to say good-bye," she whispered.

"Good-bye?" I said, setting her down and wiping her cheek. "I'm not going anywhere. We're going to figure this out together."

"I will not have this many potential civilian casualties here while we sort this," Nicole barked. But I only had eyes for Rosi's relieved grin.

"Jackson already okayed it," I said, holding up the weapon he'd given me without breaking eye contact.

Rosi cleared her throat and cocked her hip while honing in on her friend. "Cora, you should go. Austin's here for me, I'll be fine. But I might not if I'm worried about where you are and if you're safe."

Cora blew a section of rainbow hair from her face and crossed her arms. "I might be helpful, you know. I can ask for help from my guides in locating this thing."

Everyone looked at Nicole, who turned away and pressed a finger to her ear, listening to something none of us could hear. When she spun back to us, she had a grim look on her face.

"Well, you three successfully waited long enough for the emergency evacuation flights to take off. So no matter my thoughts on the subject, you are stuck here until one of the planes returns."

Cora jumped and clapped, and I shook my head, unable to marry the childish excitement with the scene I'd just witnessed in the medcenter.

Then again, Cora had yet to see the thing for herself. I hoped for hers and Rosi's sakes that wouldn't change.

25

ROSI

"ARE THE STAFF STILL HERE? OR HAVE THEY BEEN EVACUATED TOO?" I asked, ready to get down to business.

"They are the last to leave and will be here until the next plane arrives, which will be in approximately five hours." Nicole glanced at her wristcom and flipped her golden hair over a shoulder.

"I need to talk to Ila and Toklo," I said, already headed for the tubes.

"I'm coming with you," Austin said from my side. I had the feeling he'd just volunteered to be my bodyguard for the rest of the trip. I was not about to complain.

"We should all go," Nicole said. "There's strength in numbers."

"Wait!" Cora yelled and spun around to run back in the room. She emerged in moments with her deck of worn Tarot cards and a satchel that read, *Go Sage Yourself*. "Okay. Ooh, wait. Rosi, do you still have those crystals I stuck in your bag?"

I grinned, holding up the obsidian I'd been carrying in my own bag since getting back from the excursion into hell. "I have this one. It's what saved our asses, thanks to you."

Cora immediately scrounged in her sack until she came back up with a handful of black stones. She handed some to Nicole and some to Austin then stuffed the rest in her neon-pink bra that glowed like a beacon under her netted crop top.

"What does it do?" Nicole asked, holding her handful in front of her like medicine she didn't trust.

"Protection from negative energy," Cora said, leading the way to the tubes. "You can scoff if you want, but if it helped save their lives, there's obviously something to it."

"I didn't scoff," Nicole said as we rode down to the now empty first floor.

Cora glanced over her shoulder. "I felt it."

Holding a hand out, I stopped Nicole's retort before it came. I knew Cora, and she loved a challenge. We needed to stay focused. Besides, she wasn't wrong. Whatever quality was in the obsidian had sent the beast running.

Beast. I'd been digging through my books and materials on Inuit culture since leaving Austin's side. It was the only way not to relive the horrible moment of the claw shredding his arm over and over again. I thought I'd found the answer, but I needed confirmation from an expert.

The sound of the rushing waterfall gave way as I led our group to the museum. In its place, Nicole's heels tapped at the ground like tiny icepicks and Cora shuffled her cards. The glowing, blue emergency lights gave an eerie feel to the empty halls, and I hurried forward until we finally arrived.

When the doors slid open, I found Ila sitting on the counter in the center of her own hologram. Yuka jumped up from the floor where she lay at Toklo's feet and pranced over to sniff and greet us. The mother and son were so entrenched in conversation, they didn't notice our intrusion until she barked.

Ila's eyes met mine then swiftly looked away as she hopped down to meet us. "Shouldn't you be on the way back to California?" she asked with a strained smile.

"Not until I help figure this out," I said. Then I put a hand on her shoulder and leaned in. "I need your help identifying what we're dealing with."

Pressing her lips closed, Ila's gaze fell somewhere over my shoulder. I turned back to see what she was looking at and gasped.

The AC glass bubble in the back corner display had shattered—something it shouldn't have been able to do. Tiny specks of broken glass twinkled in the blue light from above, and the space, previously occupied by the horrifying totem I'd seen, was now empty.

I spun back to face Ila. "Someone stole the piece your great-grandfather made!"

Toklo placed a hand on his mother's shoulder, and she seemed to relax. "We don't know what happened." I felt like he was trying to tell me something more but couldn't figure it out, especially with those around me.

"I'm sorry about your great-grandfather's work," Nicole said gently. "But right now, we have an emergency on our hands.

"You all need to go," Ila said. "It's going to take all my time to pack up these things properly."

"Leave them," Nicole said. "We will reopen as soon as this issue is resolved."

"No offense, Miss Bennet, but we'd feel safer leaving with our things. We aren't sure that many of your tourists are interested in this part of the resort anyway." Toklo stepped in front of his mother protectively and ushered everyone toward the door.

"*Atshen*," I said, and he froze. His mother gasped, throwing a hand to her mouth.

I guess I have my answer then.

"What's that mean?" Austin asked.

I considered how to explain it. "Ever heard of a wendigo? It's similar. It starts out as a human, but it turns to cannibalism, which turns it into... Well, into what got inside the resort." I shuddered.

"This is ridiculous," Nicole said, throwing up her hands. "Sabotage I believe in, but monsters?"

"It's real," Ila said, deflating before our eyes. "When Toklo told me what happened, what kind of injuries you had, I knew it to be true."

Yuka whined, and I reached down to pat her head. Even the dogs believed it. They knew before we did.

I sighed, continuing to pet the dog. "When we crashed, we found shelter in a set of natural catacombs. There had been others there before us, and I don't know if he was one of them who resorted to eating the rest because of starvation, or if he was already here and they were unaware, but all that's left is a pile of their things and a pile of their bones."

"That's horrible," Nicole said.

I nodded. "But that's how I figured it out. That, its appearance, and the way it went at Austin."

"I'm not turning into a werewolf or anything, am I?" Austin asked, wide-eyed.

Laughing felt ridiculously good under the circumstances. "No. Not that dating an alpha wolf would be so bad, but as long as you don't start eating humans, we're okay."

"*Anaq!*" Toklo swore, and Ila glared at him. "Tell them," he begged.

"Tell us what?" Nicole asked, pushing between us.

Cora plopped down on the ground and hummed, laying out cards in a semi-circle. Austin knelt to play with Yuka. It was like they wanted to pretend they weren't part of this conversation, and I couldn't blame either of them.

"We think," Ila began, glancing at me over Nicole's shoulder, "the outcast the *tupilaq* was created to seek out is the creature you seek."

I paled as the story she'd told me came rushing back. The murderer. The pedophile. The man that disappeared into the tundra. He'd spoken to me—toyed with me like a serial killer would. And what had he said? *Almost as good as a young one.*

"I'm going to be sick," I said behind my hand. Toklo took my arm and walked me to the office, where he helped me into a chair.

Behind us, Ila retold the story to Nicole and the others. As hard of a time as Nicole was having with believing this, I was already certain it was the truth.

"He was a monster, and he turned into a literal one," I said as Toklo squatted beside me, letting loose a huge lungful of air.

"I grew up hearing stories about him from my father," he said. "Mom hated it and always scolded him for scaring me. Never thought he was real."

Boy, did I know what that felt like. "So any idea what can stop an *atshen*?" I asked.

Toklo shook his head, mouth pursed as he considered. "Well, according to the stories, a *tupilaq*. The one that was created to kill him specifically is now missing from the museum. Not that it was doing its job anyway."

"That thing gave me the creeps, to be honest," I said. "The way it's made maybe? I don't know exactly, but is there another way to make one?"

Toklo grinned up at me. "No, but that's one of the many reasons I decided not to follow in Great-grandad's footsteps."

"Do you have abilities?" I asked, swiveling toward him, surprised at his admission.

He shrugged. "Supposedly, my family inherits it. But all I ever got was a dream predicting Yuka."

A smile tugged at my lips. "You dreamed her?"

"Yeah." Toklo brushed at his hair. "I dreamed I'd find a pure-white pup, and the next day I caught her following me through the village. Not that surprising though since I was picking up fish for dinner."

"Hey!" Cora called from the other room. "Get in here!"

Toklo and I rushed back in, fear gripping my stomach. But the look on Cora's face was excitement and not terror as she stared down at her cards.

"What is it?" Nicole asked, and it could have been my imagination, but she seemed frazzled for the first time since I'd met her.

"I did a line for each of us," Cora said, indicating three columns of six cards each.

"Is that shit safe?" Toklo asked.

"I always protect spiritually first," Cora said. "But this isn't the interesting part." She poked a finger toward a second, small pile of cards face up in front of us.

I squinted as she spread them apart so we could see each individual one. It was the Devil, the Seven of Swords, the Wheel of Fortune, and a card I was quite familiar with—the Tower.

"What does that mean?" Nicole asked, narrowing her eyes.

Cora pointed to each card in turn as she explained her interpretation. "He's the devil, trapped in the need for material and physical gratification without thought of the consequences. He's used to using deception and plans trickery."

"Great," Austin said, leaning back on his hands.

Cora continued, unphased. "His luck is about to change because the wheel of fortune always turns, and—"

"Pretty much death and destruction," I finished for her. "I got that card before our excursion." I almost said I should have listened, and I'd never wished this on anyone, but the truth was, part of me celebrated that I'd gone, despite the circumstances. It had let me reconnect with Austin.

"But is that death and destruction he brings, or death and destruction for him?" Toklo asked, bending over the cards and reaching out a hand like he wanted to touch them, equally afraid and drawn to them.

Cora furrowed her brow, scooped up the cards, and began shuffling again.

"When will it strike next?" Nicole asked me, grasping my shoulder. Apparently, she needed to hear things from a scientific perspective. At least she trusted me as an expert. But the truth was, I only knew what I'd read and what Ila and Toklo had shared.

I shrugged, feeling ill. "I'd like to think eating an entire human would keep him full for a while. But you should know my research says he'll grow with each body he consumes."

Cora grimaced.

"He was already like eight feet tall," Austin said, standing. "And there weren't that many people to eat out there."

We stared at each other for a while, no one willing to comment on that observation.

"How do we get rid of it?" Nicole finally broke the silence.

"We don't," Ila said. "We get the fuck out of here and call it a loss. I'm sorry, Miss Bennet, but that's the truth."

Nicole rose to her full height, which although wasn't over five foot four, still made her feel intimidating. "I am not letting a sick, cannibalistic pedophile scare me off my resort. I don't care if it's human or something else. If it breaths, I can kill it."

I believed she could.

Her wristcom beeped. "Nicole! Location!" Jackson shouted through the speaker.

"Museum," she responded calmly, holding it up to her mouth.

Before she lowered her wrist, the door opened, and a crazed-looking Jackson rushed through, his wide-eyed face splattered with blood.

Nicole hurried to his side. "Babe, are you okay?"

He shook his head as he took her in his arms. "Carter isn't. We were cleaning up the room and had the AI searching for clues. It located biological matter inside the air ducts. I took Carter and Yang to search the area, and we found a stack of broken bones. They had bite marks all over them."

The sheer willpower it took not to scream, vomit, or run out the door was incredible.

"The blood?" Nicole asked, searching his eyes as she ran a manicured finger down his cheek.

Jackson looked away. "The creature came out of nowhere. I think it had some sort of cloaking technology. Before I could raise my gun, it had ripped his arm out."

I fell back into Austin's waiting embrace and buried my face in his chest. But the comfort he provided didn't stop me from seeing it all in my mind's eye.

"Yang and I shot at it, and it yanked off Carter's other arm before running off with it. Yang is trying to fix Carter up in what's left of the medcenter. I've never seen anything like this, Nikki."

"Do you think you wounded it?" Nicole asked, her voice smaller than I'd ever heard.

Jackson shook his head. "No. I think I upset it. But as far as I could tell, the lasers had little effect other than an annoyance."

"Shit," Nicole said, pulling her own laser pistol and glaring at it like it had disappointed her.

"We need blades," Toklo said, bending over Cora. We turned to him as he dropped a card from the top of the deck. The Ace of Swords fluttered down and landed at his feet. He pulled another, and the Knight of Swords fell on top of it.

Maybe his shaman bloodline worked with Cora's cards. Maybe the others would call it a coincidence, but either way it made sense.

"We don't have swords," Nicole said as though coming to the same conclusion.

"We have hunting tools though," Ila said, rushing to open an exhibit filled with old yet wicked-looking weaponry. "They aren't made of obsidian, but they'll have to do."

Silently, she handed out knives, spears, and a large, scary-looking hook to her son. I got something like a dagger, which might be easier to handle but worried me when I thought of how close I'd have to be to those teeth to use it. The creature's incisors were longer than the blade, and while they were thinner, there were far too many of them.

26

AUSTIN

THE DOOR *SWISHED* OPEN, AND I SPUN AROUND, SPEAR HOISTED OVER my shoulder and ready. But it was a human at the door, a woman covered in blood. The coppery scent immediately brought me back to the room where the doc had been killed.

"Yang! Where's Carter?" Jackson asked, forcing some clarity in the woman's wide-unfocused eyes.

She wrung her hands as she spoke. "I put him in stasis. I couldn't stop the blood. It was like whatever substance was in that thing's teeth prevented it from clotting even with the tech in medcenter. It was the best I could do to stop him from dying until someone with more know-how can get to him."

None of us mentioned that he was a sitting duck. Or that she probably did the smart thing by finding us instead of staying behind. The way she refused to meet anyone's eyes indicated the guilt she felt over her decision, but who could blame her?

Clearing my throat, I stepped forward, spear at my side. "What's our objective? We all need to agree and be clear on this."

"Hunt it and kill it," Nicole said while at the same time, Rosi said, "Survive."

They looked at each other with wide eyes.

"So the question is," I clarified, "Do we go on the offensive, or do we find a defensible place to hold up?"

"We don't even know we can kill it," Toklo said.

"Then why did the cards tell us to arm ourselves with these?" Cora asked, rising with her hands on her hips to face him.

"And the gun didn't hurt him, but it did scare him off. At least for now," Yang said, moving in farther to join the conversation.

This was all good. Instead of panicking, they rose to the challenge. Focusing on the problems in the now would get us out of this, just as I'd been taught.

"When trapped in Paradise Atlantis, we got out of the situation by acting on it," Nicole said. "I'm not sitting around, waiting to be attacked by a cannibalistic monster. The rest of you do what you want until the next plane returns." She headed for the door with Jackson rushing to keep up.

"Stop," Rosi said, and Nicole swung around, eyes narrowed. "You can't just walk away."

"I own this resort. It's not only my responsibility, but I am also the best qualified to deal with the situation."

I winced, expecting Rosi or any other reasonable human being to cower at Nicole's attitude. Instead, Rosi drew herself up to her full height and continued talking before Nicole could turn around.

"I read about what happened—everything I could get my hands on before I came," Rosi said. "You and Jackson ended up in stasis along with everyone else. It was your brother and an engineering student that made it to the surface to get help."

Based on Nicole's red face and murderous gaze, maybe things weren't going as swimmingly as I first thought. I put an arm around Rosi in support.

"Be that as it may," Nicole said, sharing her venom with me as well. "We were the last caught, and we did it for the good of the group. We knew the risks then and we know them now. But I'll still be damned if I'm going to sit down and hide when I may be able to do something. I'm not asking you to come if you aren't up for it. I appreciate your help clarifying what we're up against. It seems likely to attack again in the medcenter, so that's where we head."

Rosi's entire body tensed, but her mouth snapped closed. Nicole, Jackson, and Yang exited the room. Apparently, Nicole had come to the same conclusion I had about Carter being a sitting duck, and I hoped they'd get there in time. Meanwhile, I had four other people I felt responsible for gathered here in the museum.

"What are you thinking?" Rosi asked, slipping her hand in mine.

"Just going over scenarios in my head. It's one of the things I do when I'm prepping for an event," I said, squeezing her fingers for reassurance.

"I kind of agree with Miss Bennet." Toklo stroked Yuka's soft fur. "At least the part about not waiting around for something to happen. But I'm not so sure about killing the thing."

"I get it," I said, placing a hand on his shoulder. "Hunting is one sport I've never participated in. But if it comes to self-defense..."

Cora frowned, shuffling her cards again. I wondered if they acted as a sort of fidget toy for her since she seemed to be doing it without paying attention.

She said, "I think that's why the cards said to take sharp objects. I don't think they meant for us to seek it out and attack it."

"He has to die." Ila's soft yet stern voice made us all turn to face the back of the room, where she'd been sitting quietly, taking it all in.

Brushing past my side, Rosi crossed over to her and squatted so she could look up into the woman's face. The slight tremble in Ila's hand on the edge of the information kiosk left little doubt as to how affected she was by the circumstances.

"Is it because of the totem your great-grandfather made?" Rosi asked gently.

Ila met her gaze and shook her head slowly. "It should have worked. He swore it would work."

Cora and I exchanged glances as Toklo rushed to his mother's side.

"There's more to the story than you told, isn't there?" Cora asked. She split her deck and held up the exposed card. It was titled, *The Empress* in scrawling gold letters.

Ila's bottom lip trembled, and she turned her head away from everyone. "The rest of the story doesn't matter. You know what he did and what he continues to do. He deserves death."

"You keep referring to the monster as a 'he' even though he's changed," I said.

"Stop pushing her!" Toklo got in my face so fast, if I hadn't been so good at balancing, my momentum would've taken us both down. Yuka whined and placed her paws over her head.

I threw my hands up, palms out, and took a step back. "Just trying to get all the information in case something helps."

Eyes flashing—and I could have sworn I saw red for a second— Toklo crossed his arms over his chest, exposing his large, tatted biceps. While I had no desire to fight him, I knew my years of training would give me the advantage if need be.

"Look, it doesn't matter." Rosi stood and slipped between us. "If the *atshen* comes for us, it's not like we'd stop to chat. It will attack as it always has, and we will defend ourselves to the best of our ability."

"Should we stay here?" Toklo asked, watching his mother for cues.

"We have to find the *tupilaq*," Ila said with conviction. "It will kill him as my grandfather intended."

Did she really think anything small enough to fit in that busted case capable of killing an eight-feet-tall monster? I glanced at Rosi, silently asking if the woman was nuts. But Rosi was nodding her agreement.

"Do you think he took it?" Rosi asked.

Ila laughed bitterly. "No. He's evil, but he's not stupid."

"Are you saying this *atshen* has intelligence?" Cora asked, drawing closer.

"It spoke in my mind," Rosi said. She wouldn't meet my eyes. "When it attacked us outside. It taunted me, and I understood every word."

"Shit, Rosi. I'm so sorry." I went to comfort her, or maybe to comfort us both.

"Then who took the *tupilaq*?" Cora asked.

"Maybe some kids stole it during the evacuation?" Toklo offered.

"No." Ila stood. "I was in my office when it happened. An alarm sounds when someone comes in, so I know to check if I can assist them. No one came in. I ran out the door the second the glass shattered. I'd have seen someone leaving."

"That means it has to still be here somewhere!" Rosi pulled away from me and rushed back to the mess in the corner.

"It's not," Ila said. "I checked. The truth is, I think the *tupilaq* sensed him here because he was so close and went after him."

"You think it's been waiting all this time to fulfill its mission?" Rosi asked, still peering around the area. "That the *atshen's* presence activated it?"

Ila nodded. "Toklo can find the *tupilaq*."

"Me?" Her son's voice was so high-pitched I winced.

"You have the gift."

"*Anaq*," he swore beneath his breath again.

"I'll help you." Cora clapped then reached in her satchel and dug around, coming back up with a pyramid made of clear quartz, which she handed to him. "Here. To focus your energy."

Toklo took it gingerly and stared at it. "Now what?"

"Ask the ancestors to guide you to the *tupilaq*," Ila said as Rosi sat beside her.

"Take a deep breath," I offered. "Focus on it going through your body and out again."

Closing his eyes, Toklo made a face of intense focus, and we collectively held our breath. After a few tense minutes, his eyelids snapped open, and the red I'd caught a glimpse of earlier shone through his irises before dimming into a normal shade of brown.

"I don't know how to explain this, but I'm supposed to go up to the anti-grav track."

"Let's do it," I said, antsy to do something more than talk.

"Ila must not go." Toklo pointed at his mother, but it wasn't his voice that came from between his lips. It was that of an old man, deep and crackly.

Throwing a hand to her chest, Ila gasped and reeled back. Rosi put an arm around her shoulders. "I'll stay with you."

"I'll stay too then," I said.

"Toklo will need assistance," the old man voice said again, circling to point Toklo's finger in my direction. "The women are safer here."

"Fuck that, old man ancestor!" Cora shouted. "I'm coming too."

27

ROSI

I supposed I should've thanked Austin for being gallant when he offered to stay behind. Instead, I wanted to yell at him. In Spanish. It was Ila's hand on my arm that made me stop and take a breath.

"Why are you so angry?" Austin furrowed his brow. "Don't you want to stay together?"

"Of course I do! But you heard the ancestor—you're needed. Do you really think it's a good idea to ignore the warning of the spirit taking over someone's body?" The moment those words crossed my lips, I felt weak in the knees.

My whole life had been spent hiding these very thoughts from others and tiptoeing around things to make them more palatable. Here I was, finally able to speak freely with others who'd witnessed things as well, so why was I filled with so much rage? The answer drained away the anger and made me want to sink to the floor.

I didn't want to separate from Austin. I wanted to stay together as much as he did, but I knew that was selfish. The truth was, I was scared shitless, and I'd asked for this.

"I agree. Austin should come," Cora said, and I could have hugged her for backing me up because I was so close to changing my own mind. "But, Rosi, you don't have to stay here just because an old man told you to."

"I'm not leaving Ila alone." It wouldn't be right. And I wanted to know what she wasn't saying, because I had a feeling there was more.

"Ila must stay," the spirit repeated. "Or it will confuse the *tupilaq.*"

I very much wanted to find out exactly why that would be. But I sensed Ila wasn't going to be forthcoming in front of everyone else —especially her son.

"We stay, the rest of you go find it and figure out what needs to happen next," I said.

Austin's glare was made of ice, and I wondered if I'd somehow made a mistake by insisting he go when we both wanted to be together. But logically, it made sense. If logic could still play a part in any of this. He hesitated at the door even as Toklo and Cora headed out, Toklo, stopping at a case to the side of the room and removing a large staff or walking stick.

I hurried over to Austin, intending to kiss him good-bye for now. But when I touched the taught muscles in his arms, I stepped back. I'd never seen him so upset.

"I'll never forgive myself if something happens to you," he said.

Then my own anger flared once again. "This isn't about you, Austin. I'm an adult. I am choosing to stay here with Ila." And it was a damned hard decision too.

"Shouldn't I get a choice too?" he asked, his eyes tornadoes that stole the air from my lungs.

"I don't need a babysitter."

"Neither does Ila."

Aaahhh! This man drove me insane. I shoved him in the stubbornly solid chest and stormed back to sit by Ila, refusing to acknowledge him further. Didn't he know how hard this was on me? We had to do what was best for everyone.

I didn't look up again until the door *swished* shut behind him.

"He's controlling," Ila said.

"He's used to making split-second, life or death decisions," I said, dropping my shoulders.

"He'll learn to let others take the lead. Thank you for staying, but you didn't have to." Ila patted my hand and smiled at me.

"You're welcome. I know I wouldn't want to be alone," I said.

"You want to ask me about it."

Nodding, I felt a blush warm my cheeks. She laughed at me, but it was a good-natured guffaw that finally had me relaxing all over. Having a bloodthirsty monster out to get me really stressed me out. That had to be what was going on with Austin too.

"You with all your questions. I should have figured you'd get it all out of me at some point. My husband says I should write a book. I don't have the patience for it."

"You might feel better if you tell me the whole story," I offered. "I promise I'll believe you."

"I know." Ila grinned then sighed, readjusting herself to face me comfortably. "It was my grandfather, not my great-grandfather that made the *tupilaq*."

"Why lie about that?" I asked, wishing I had my notebook handy to jot the story down.

Shrugging, she continued. "The *atshen*'s name was Yutu when he was human. Yutu was a prominent man in the village, but there had always been stories about him. The idea of visiting his home made my mother's skin crawl as a child. He was a master hunter, so he provided much-needed food for the village. That's why they let him get away with it for so long, turning their heads when he took the young girls overnight. He didn't do it often, but once a year or so was enough to be noticed, and the girls were never the same after. He took my mother's friend Alasie, and she barely spoke a word after that."

I cringed at the idea of the man using his position of power to abuse young girls. It was the kind of story that happened in all cultures and across all times. Sick people hurt others. I squeezed her hand as I digested the story.

"She begged my grandfather to do something after Alasie. He was the village *angakukk* and so was supposed to protect us all, but unlike the rest of our ancestors, he was far too concerned with his own comfort and pride—things he should have forgone to embrace the title of *angakukk*. He said he wouldn't lift a hand against Yutu, and to be honest my mother said he seemed afraid of the hunter. It wasn't just my mother asking though. It was many of the villagers, including the parents of those taken by Yutu over the years."

Visions of angry villagers with pitchforks swam in my brain, though I knew that wasn't quite accurate. Still, the anger they would have felt and the need for justice... I leaned in farther, encouraging her to continue.

"It was Alasie's father who took my mother to Yutu. She told him she wanted to help bring the man to justice, so he felt justified in delivering her on a platter. My mother was beautiful even then and had barely gotten her first blood. Her *kakiniit* were still raw." Ila indicated her own chin tattoos. "Alasie's father tied Mother to the pole in front of Yutu's house and tore off her clothing. She nearly froze to death by the time he discovered her and brought her in before his fire."

I shivered and knew the horror must have shown clearly on my face.

Ila nodded. "He kept her hands tied. She didn't tell me the details, but she had scars on her abdomen she kept covered until her death years later. She said she'd never forget his laugh whenever she cried in pain. And she knew what her friend had gone through. When he was done with her, he put her in an old *anorak* and sent her on her way."

A single tear trailed down Ila's cheek, and I squeezed her hand harder.

"I'm so sorry," I whispered. "Was that when your grandfather made the *tupilaq*?"

"No. But it was when he banished Yutu to the frozen wasteland out this way. Alasie's father had understood that he would act when it became personal enough for him."

"I get why you hate him so much," I said quietly. "At least your mother was able to marry and have you—she moved on."

Ila's laugh morphed into a terrible cry, and I froze, wondering what I'd said wrong. But she didn't pull away, and I let her get it out, waiting patiently for her explanation.

"No, she never married. I was born nine months later, and it was on that day that the first victim was left at the door of my grandfather's home."

My hands flew to my mouth to cover my reaction.

"It was an eight-year-old girl. She was naked, and parts of her were missing. Two more bodies were discovered as the year continued. No one could understand how he survived, even as great of a huntsman as he was. That's when my grandfather created the *tupilaq*. But now I know it never found him because he was no longer human. He must've eaten some of the victims and traveled out this way, turning into the *atshen*."

My head pounded and my body trembled as I considered the story I'd just heard. Ila's lip curled in a sarcastic smile. "You can go find your boyfriend now. He was right to want you to leave me here. I'm the daughter of a monster. I was created out of pain. I never told my husband the truth about me, just my mother's story. And he, like you, assumed a different ending."

I shook my head and licked my very dry lips as I considered my next words. "Ila, you aren't a monster. You are the beautiful diamond that came from the coal. We—neither one of us—are our parents. We make our own choices and have our own beliefs."

Ila's eyes overflowed with tears. "Please don't tell Toklo. He is a good man. If he were to become an *angakukk*, he'd be a good one and do the right thing, unlike my grandfather."

"I won't tell him. That's up to you. But know that it changes nothing. Just like he's amazing, so are you."

"Then why would the *tupilaq* attack me by mistake? That's what grandfather warned of."

Grandfather? The old man's voice that came from Toklo must've been recognizable to her. He was the maker.

"It's only the blood in your veins, not the intent of your heart," I said, certain of it. "It was made to attack the man Yutu had been, not the monster he unleashed."

Ila pulled me in and hugged me with so much force I nearly coughed. But I rocked with her, back and forth, until she was satisfied.

"Thank you, Rosi."

I nodded, now more inclined to join Nicole on her murder quest. But perhaps in his own quest for survival at all costs, Yutu had succeeded in punishing himself worse than a quick death would have provided. It seemed that tragedy begot tragedy with one bad act leading to a mountain of them.

It was then it occurred to me that if Ila's blood was a problem, that would mean her son's would be as well. But I bit down on a chunk of my hair to prevent myself making that observation out loud. Surely, Ila's grandfather would have known this. Perhaps that was why he joined with Toklo.

Thinking about the others brought my mind back to Austin and how he'd reluctantly left. I resolved to be careful about losing my temper in the future and doing something I'd regret. I just hoped that whatever was happening up there, he'd be able to focus.

28

AUSTIN

FRUSTRATION AND FEAR MADE A DISTRACTING COCKTAIL, BUT I TRIED my best to breathe through it. In the short time I'd known her, Rosi had become an expert at pushing my buttons—the good ones and the not so good. Part of me wanted to throw her over my knee and spank her, but that part also longed to have her do the same, so I doubted it was about domination more than sexual play and experimentation. I wanted to try everything with her. If only she didn't make me want to tear my hair out in the meantime.

"How do we get up there?" Cora asked, craning her neck to see the uppermost dome of the resort. "Are the tubes working?"

"I climbed the rocks last time," I said with a shrug.

"Well, that's not exactly practical for the rest of us," she said with a snort.

Toklo raised his staff in the air, his eyes glowing red. Cora and I fell silent. In moments, the sound of something cutting through the air rushed toward us. I tackled Cora, knocking her to the ground as a slew of hover disks soared past, stopping in front of Toklo.

He stepped on a pair and rose into the air, not acknowledging that he'd nearly amputated us below the knees.

Cora huffed and stood, selecting two disks of her own, and I followed suit. Balancing wasn't an issue for me. I'd used the earliest version of these as a kid. Cora on the other hand, stumbled and nearly fell off, so I grabbed her arm to steady her.

"Thanks," she said, and when she glanced at me, moisture glistened in her eyes. "You're a good guy, Austin. I hope we don't get eaten and you and Rosi get a happy-ever-after."

I smiled. "We all will, Cora," I promised. "I've been in tight spots before. You want to know the trick?"

Cora nodded as I guided us slowly upward, careful to keep her concentration on my face in case she freaked out about the floor rapidly falling away below us. The real danger was at the top, not below.

"The trick is to let go of the fear and be in the moment," I said. "Fear is a weapon that monster uses against us because all we're thinking about is a possible future—and a negative one at that. What we need to focus on is what is actually happening and let the future come."

Cora smiled. "You sound like the spiritual guru I listen to on this one holo."

"She sounds pretty smart," I said, making Cora giggle as we reached the track.

I half-expected the monster to be waiting, but it was quiet.

We hopped off our disks and waited, looking around as Toklo kept his eyes closed, staff at the ready.

"Now what?" Cora whispered.

"We have come to guide you as requested," Toklo said then pounded the bottom of his staff on the ground.

A thunderous boom shook the entire track, and Cora stumbled before grasping the green crystal around her neck and whispering something to herself. I had a feeling it was either a prayer or a string of cuss words, or possibly both.

The starlit sky above the dome seemed to darken, and the emergency lights glowed sapphire, illuminating the space. It made my companions faces appear sickly. A new sound rose in the space surrounding us, a rush of intense of air. It felt like being in the center of a cyclone, or at least what I imagined that to be like as the wind spun around us. It kicked up a tornado of debris which swirled without touching us. Metal groaned as the storm pried a section of the safety railing from its spot and whipped it around us so fast it would prove deadly should anyone step into the whirlwind.

Cora screamed as it grew larger, reaching outward and upward and straining against the AC glass of the enclosure. If this thing shattered the dome like it had the display case, we'd all die from exposure.

"Stop!" I yelled to the storm, unsure to whom I spoke. "You'll kill everyone here except the monster."

The glass of the enclosure settled with an audible creak as the wind dropped in intensity. But rather than relax, my breathing quickened, and I backed toward the edge of the broken railing as the debris swirled together to form an enormous face. It was the type I'd seen on art and artifacts, like a ceremonial mask with giant black eyes and teeth.

The face tilted down toward me, and I sank into a ready stance, unsure what I could do if it attacked.

The ground beneath me shook when it spoke. "You have brought me the one I seek?"

"We don't know where it is, but it's in this resort somewhere," I said.

"I smell him here," the voice yelled, and the gust that blew across my face had me ducking to avoid being blown off my feet.

Toklo's body rose into the air before the giant eyes. "This man will die."

"It isn't him!" Cora yelled to be heard "The man you seek is an *atshen* now. That's why you couldn't find him."

Toklo's body crumpled to the floor when it released him, and the face turned to Cora. "Where is the one I seek?"

Cora snorted, startling me. Maybe she was losing it. "Some

spirit hunter you are," she said, laughing louder. "My friends practically led him to you, and you still want our help."

Narrowing my eyes, I sent Cora the strongest mental message I could: *Don't piss off the giant face made of wind.*

But the face leaned toward her, and to her credit she didn't back away. I guess my talk on the way up helped. "Your friends led him to me by my own design. None of this has been accidental. It has been orchestrated by me over the years and with the help of my master's kin. Now tell me where he is so I may finally rest."

Cora stumbled from the power behind the last sentence, and I rushed to her side to steady her.

"We don't know exactly where he is," I said. "But he is here, and we need your help surviving."

"I have one purpose and one purpose alone. I will destroy the man called Yutu, and if I must bring this building down to do so, it shall be done."

29

ROSI

PETTING YUKA HELPED ME RELAX TO THE POINT I'D ALMOST forgotten I was in mortal danger. I'd always loved animals but hadn't had one of my own since I was twelve. That was when Sparky passed over the rainbow bridge, and my ever-practical parents seemed more relieved than upset. Though they let me place his picture on the altar during *Dia De Los Muertos*, they'd never agreed to get another pet.

Why was I thinking of my parents?

The ground beneath us jolted, and before I could catch a breath, the entire world shook. Artifacts tumbled down around me as Ila dropped beside me on the floor, screaming. I hugged Yuka to me and put my other arm over my head.

"It's okay, Ila, it's just an earthquake," I yelled, trying to calm her. Living in California made me a pro at handling these situations, though my body still went into fight-or-flight mode with the adrenaline rush.

This was a long earthquake.

The ones I'd experienced lasted all of ten seconds, maybe twenty. This had to be going on thirty or forty.

Panic gripped me as I released Yuka and crawled along the ground toward the doorway. "Come with me."

I prayed silently that the architects had designed this resort with some solid foundations and an earthquake-proof design. Was that part of the laws when building in Greenland? Nicole seemed like a lot of things, but a woman who cut corners wasn't one of them.

The rumbling stopped when we reached the doors, but the room was in shambles, save the AC glass which held together well, making the missing *tupilaq* an even bigger issue in my mind.

The doors had jammed partially open so that only a very petite person could squeeze through sideways. I doubted I'd make it without getting stuck, but Yuka ran straight through and down the corridor.

"Yuka, wait!" I called, but her barks had dimmed to barely audible by the time I got the words out.

"We're trapped," Ila said, eyes wild with panic. She grabbed my arm a bit too tightly, and I yanked it back.

"We'll be fine. It's okay, Ila. But I need you to stay calm."

"This is all my fault," she said as I tried hard not to react to her frightened expression.

"None of this is your fault. We don't even know what that was," I said as evenly and slowly as I could. "I know this is stressful, but we are doing really well, considering."

The attempted smile fell from my face as she shook her head of raven hair back and forth. "No, I'm an abomination." She burst into sobs. "It's come for me, finally. The *tupilaq* demands payment."

This time I grabbed her arms and shook her to get her to look at me. "No one is going after anyone except the *atshen*. Whatever it is or whoever it used to be is no longer human. Do you understand? You are not responsible for the sins of your father."

Ila gulped down air, and I did not release my hold on her until she'd mostly quieted.

Then she looked away. "I'm sorry. I've embarrassed myself."

"You've done nothing wrong," I reiterated. "You've been through more than anyone should have to in a lifetime. But you're going to get out of here with your son."

"Rosi!" Austin's voice was like warm sunshine on a winter's day.

My heart leaped. I reached through the door to touch his face as we both sank to our knees.

"Thank God you're all right," he said, drawing me toward him to kiss me through the opening.

"What happened?" I asked when he pulled away.

He tucked a stray hair behind my ear which promptly boinged out again. I waited, hoping to hear him tell me it was all over, but the longer he hesitated, the faster my heart beat.

"Where are Cora and Toklo?" I asked, straining to look around him to the hall. "Austin?"

He held my face in his hands, gray eyes like clouds blocking the sun. "They're still at the track."

"Are they—they aren't—" I couldn't get myself to say the word I feared most.

"No, they aren't dead," he said quickly, and I relaxed a bit. "But it's hard to explain. The spirit thing came to us, and it is willing to destroy the whole resort to get to the monster. We need to bring it to him."

"Where is my son?" Ila cut in, pressing against my shoulder to make room for herself in the conversation.

Austin licked his lips. "That thing—"

"The *tupilaq*," I corrected.

Austin nodded. "It's now a giant wind face. It wasn't so willing to wait to destroy everyone."

"That was the earthquake," I said, realizing what had nearly happened.

"Right. Well, it only agreed to give me a few more hours to bring it the monster in exchange for leaving the others up there." He bit his bottom lip and looked away.

"You're leaving something out, Austin," I said, knowing he was holding back. "What is it?"

He sighed, his shoulders slumping. "It... He said he would work on strengthening his energy in preparation for dealing with this monster once and for all. Apparently, Toklo and Cora are gifted, and he's able to draw energy from them."

Ila fell back on her knees, in shock.

Dizzy with worry, I grabbed Austin's hand. "Is he going to drain them? Is he killing them, Austin?"

Shaking his head, Austin gripped me right back. "That's the time limit, Rosi. They have about three hours' worth of energy, apparently, and if I can't get that monster up there by then, we all die. Well, those of us still here do, so the first thing we have to do is evacuate everyone else."

"Agreed," I said, and he seemed to visibly relax. "Help me get this door open."

Austin stood and braced himself, using raw strength to pull the door open another few inches—enough to make the difference and allow us to climb through. I fell into his arms and reveled for a selfish moment in the comfort that brought.

Pressing my head to his chest, I took strength from his steady heartbeat and said, "You should go tell Nicole and the others to get on their gear and wait outside for the plane."

Austin pulled away to look at me. "I will. You two get your gear on and get out there."

He turned to leave as my mind spun. "I'm not going, Austin. I'm helping with the search."

He froze, facing the other way then spoke so softly I almost didn't hear him. "I thought you agreed?"

"I did. To evacuating the others," I said, catching up so I could face him.

"We don't have time to argue about this," he said. "Cora and Toklo don't have time."

"Exactly," I said, unable to make sense of the jumble of feelings that assaulted me. "So don't. Just go tell the others to leave. I'll start the search."

"As will I," Ila said. I smiled and nodded, knowing aside from the hypocrisy of it, there'd be no way to convince her otherwise when her son was the one trapped up there being drained by a spiritual hitman.

Austin reminded me of a volcano ready to erupt. His skin flushed scarlet, and his breathing increased by the second.

"Ila, can you please give us a moment?" I asked, eyes locked on Austin.

"I'll grab a holopad and pull up a map of the ducts," she said to the sound of her retreating footsteps.

"Austin—"

"Rosi, I am asking you to listen to me because I care about you. I survive the unsurvivable for a living, and I do it because I empty my mind and focus on the moment. But I can't focus since I've been here. Since I met you." He grasped my shoulders and pulled me toward him, searching my face with desperation. "You've taken the space in my heart that I've kept vacant since losing my sister. I can't lose you too."

My heart must have leaped into my throat because it was impossible to speak. But I knew what I had to say, and I knew it could put a rift between us that might never be bridged. Part of me didn't want to do it. I'd only known the man a short time, but I felt closer and more open with him than with any other man I'd ever met. I pushed the word "love" from where it danced on the recesses of my mind because it couldn't be—not that fast. Could it? I believed in bigfoot, why not believe in insta-love?

I considered his argument for a moment. He was the expert here, and his worry for me was getting in the way of his concentration. I could understand that. But I was the expert on the mythos and the one with experience with the paranormal. We both contributed to the goal, and we ought to work together to end this and save Cora and Toklo.

It was a moot point anyway.

You know you aren't leaving Cora behind, and Austin needs to hear it for his own good.

Swallowing down the enormous lump in my throat, I raised my hands to his face, hoping it wouldn't be the last time I'd feel his coarse stubble against my skin. "Austin, that means so much to me. *You* mean so much. But you can't control every situation, and you certainly can't control me."

I watched, heart breaking as the meaning of my words washed over him. Tears burst from my eyes when I realized how much this hurt him, but I forced my way through it.

"You lost your sister because you fought against her, Austin."

The words were like knives that made him physically wince as they pierced his armor. I wasn't stupid. He'd let me in when it was hard for him to trust, and this was how I repaid that trust. But if he'd only hear the message I was trying to impart.

He backed away from me and rubbed his face with the back of his hand, refusing to meet my gaze. He nodded and rushed past me down the hall toward the medcenter.

"Austin!" My voice echoed down the corridor, but he didn't turn around. "I'm sorry," I whispered to the empty space before me. And I wondered, as my heart continued to ache like I'd torn it in two, if I might have been better off listening to him.

30

AUSTIN

Rosi hit below the belt. I should have never opened my mouth, and I understood the whole she "didn't want to be a damsel in distress thing," but this was an actual fucking monster and she was an actual fucking damsel. In distress. We were all in distress. Why did she have to bring Sara in to this? Why throw that in my face when I'd trusted her with something I'd never trusted another soul with?

I brushed the tears from my face, scrubbing it to make myself stop crying before I entered the medcenter. But as I reached for the door, the truth hit me like an avalanche. She was right. I'd told her exactly the same thing. I blamed myself for not letting Sara take the lead. Still, I was the professional here, not Rosi.

Was I the professional? I'd never come across a live monster or a spirit wind face before. But Rosi had come across one of the two. Hell, she'd been searching for them and studying them for as long as I'd been training my mind and body. I wasn't a professional—I was a fucking idiot.

I strode forward and the doors opened. Nicole and Yang sprung forward, blades drawn, but stopped short at the sight of me. The room was a shambles with the furniture and medical tools strewn about and mixed with the bloodstains on the walls. Jackson and another man lay supine with white sheets pulled up to their chins.

"What happened to Jackson?" I asked.

Nicole tucked her blade to her side. "He hit his head when the earthquake struck. Passed out. We put him in the bed thinking it was safest."

"Get your exterior gear on. Both of you," I said, moving toward the unconscious men. "I'll get these hovercot shields up so you can walk them outside with you."

Nicole's dubious look came nowhere near the emotional impact of Rosi's insistence on staying, so I forged ahead, explaining the situation as I worked while Yang ran to find some gear.

"I'd stay, but I won't leave Jackson alone," Nicole said when I finished. She locked her gaze on him, and her expression softened. "Do not let this resort go down, Austin, please. If you can save this place, I promise to sponsor whatever stunts you want for the next decade."

"I'll do my best," I said, biting my tongue instead of commenting on the people's lives still at stake.

As though she heard my thoughts, she gave me a half-smile. "And save those people too. I can't afford to lose a worker or a guest." She winked as Yang returned out of breath, her arms full of padded layers.

"Get going, Austin, and good luck." Nicole practically shoved me out the door.

I hesitated in the hallway, unsure which path to take. I could find Rosi and Ila and we could search together, or I could go on my own and cover more ground.

Stubbornly, I didn't want to face Rosi after what she'd said, so I decided on the latter. What I needed was bait. But what kind of bait? It hadn't attacked since being scared off by the gun.

What was this monster about? I thought back to the story I'd heard in the museum. He was a pedophile that prayed on young girls. Well, we didn't have any of those left here, thank goodness. But it also seemed to like to instill fear in its victims. It had taunted Rosi. It ran from the gun when those it attacked showed they'd fight back. It was a coward and a bully, and it was time to turn the tables.

31

ROSI

"We have to lure Yutu to the top of the resort," I said, pacing in front of the waterfall as its white spray sloshed against the sides of the AC glass. "But how?"

"I'll be the bait," Ila said, spreading her arms wide.

"That's not going to work," I said, appreciating her bravery. "You aren't supposed to go up there, remember? Grandfather's warning?"

Her face fell, and she sat on a rock at the base of one of the walls. "Even if we get him to come after you, how will you get up there before he reaches you?"

I looked up and had to agree. If I climbed, it would take forever and a day. "Hover disks," I said, spotting some lying at the base of the waterfall.

I'd nearly reached them when Ila screamed. I spun around to find her pointing at the rocks above. When I looked up, I found the *atshen* scaling the side of the rocks at an inhuman speed, like an arachnid with oddly bent limbs. He paused and opened his enormous mouth, revealing rows of stained teeth.

Hello, tasty morsel, he said in my mind. *You will be fun to devour.*

Gagging, I doubled over, holding my roiling stomach as he flashed pictures in my mind. Pictures of me screaming as he bit into my flesh. *I haven't played with my food in many years*, he added, showing me a vision of him ripping my clothes off and trailing his claws down my body.

"Get out of my head!" I screamed, yanking the hover disks from the ground and activating them.

"Leave her alone!" Ila yelled at the same time, and his head swung toward her. "I am your daughter."

He paused his descent, no more than twenty meters from the bottom, then dropped to the ground, landing on all fours before rising up onto two legs. Despite his twisted, lean body, he had to be ten feet tall. While his size astounded me, the unnatural look of him made me ill, like his existence was an affront to the rules of physics and hurt to look at.

"One of my girls had a girl," he said in a sibilant voice. Ila braced herself as he reached forward with a clawed hand, stopping just before her face. "I remember your mother. She was gifted to me—a lovely offering. So ripe but so innocent. Yet when I accepted her, I was run from town."

Ila spit at the floor between their feet. "You sick bastard."

He made a sound that I assumed to be a laugh as he threw his head back. "You're the bastard, *daughter*. And I am hungry—so hungry."

"You just ate," I said, balancing on the hover disks.

He whipped his head toward me and laughed again. "The more I eat, the hungrier I grow. That is my curse to bear. But I will take my time with you. You remind me of them, you know."

"You should have died. Why didn't you die?" Ila yelled, and the metal of her blade flashed in her hand as she lunged.

"Ila, no!" I screamed, but it was too late. He grabbed her wrist and twisted, forcing her to drop the weapon and fall to her knees. But he lifted her by the arm so that she dangled in the air, kicking and screaming.

"My blood runs through your veins," he said, raking a claw down her side like a zipper. Blood sprayed out. "So I cannot ingest

you. I did not die because I am immortal, and those beneath me
have no consequence. Therefore, *daughter*, you are no more than a
mistake—a parasite that grew in your mother because I should
have consumed her completely and not stopped myself from
reaching my full potential."

The handle of my own dagger felt heavy and awkward as I
raced toward them on the disks. I bent low to keep my balance and
threw the weapon as he spoke. It hit below the arm that held up Ila,
and he dropped her to the floor where she landed in a heap, a
puddle of scarlet spreading out beneath her.

"You've cost me enough, little girl. Now you will suffer and beg
for death." He collapsed in on himself so that he was bent like an
insect again. His head turned at an impossible angle, and he
opened his mouth so wide, I thought he could swallow me whole.

Leaning down to grasp the bottom of the disks for added speed,
I raced away from him as fast as I could. Seeing him wasn't necessary since I heard him scrambling along the rocks to my right as I
rose higher and higher, my eyes locked on the uppermost dome of
the resort and the brilliant diamonds twinkling through.

I was going to make it.

Then the disk beneath my left foot snapped to a stop so
abruptly that I lost my balance and fell sideways, my head down,
hair falling toward the earth as I dangled impossibly in the air, still
two stories short of my goal. My bag with my crystals slid from my
shoulder, and I watched in horror as it plummeted to the ground
below.

I rotated, coming to a stop inches from the face of my nightmares. He cocked his head to look at me and opened his jaw,
revealing what would likely be my end. I had no words left, just the
rapid rise and fall of my chest as he drew me closer. A long, gray
tongue slithered from his mouth and dragged across my cheek,
drawing a whimper from me.

"You taste like heaven," he whispered, the scratchy surface of
his tongue leaving a burning sensation on my skin.

"Please." Apparently, I wasn't beyond pleading. I'd cower if it meant preventing the worst kind of death I could conceive of.

"So easy to make you beg. It brings parts of me I thought long dead to life." He hoisted me up over his shoulder and knocked the disks from my feet. I hung over his back as my only means of escape crashed to the ground below.

I closed my eyes as we climbed, trying to prevent the vertigo from making me vomit. Then he dumped me none to gently to the ground of what I recognized as the sixth floor even through the pain in my head.

Would losing consciousness make this easier? I gave myself over to it, but my stubborn brain wouldn't shut off. Yutu slunk toward me, again on all fours in a very unnatural way.

I forced my body into motion and crab walked backward until I hit the wall. If this was it, I wasn't going down without a fight.

He sprang toward me, and I kicked out, connecting with the side of his head. He howled in pain as I scrambled to my feet and prepared to run, but he caught me by the wrist and swung me around, throwing me onto my back and knocking the wind from my lungs.

The world spun as Yutu straddled me and lifted my hand to his mouth. The vision he'd shown me came back in full clarity and I scratched at his puckered gray skin and wriggled beneath his massive form, attempting to throw him off. But he held tight. I opened my mouth in preparation to scream when the tip of the first tooth sank into the meat of my hand below my thumb. Blinded with pain, I could neither move nor make a sound as he bit deeper, slowly. He stopped as I saw the tip come through the other side of my own palm.

My venom prevents my prey from moving or calling for help, but you'll feel every tiny bit. And don't worry, if you black out, I'll wake you again. You deserve no less for striking me.

Internally, I continued to struggle against him, but it was no use. He'd already injected his venom in my body, the one that Yang had said caused the blood not to clot. With any luck, he'd bleed me to death before he realized it because as he plunged more teeth into my wrist and forearm, the pain became unbearable.

A bright-blue light cut through the air and hit Yutu in the side of the face. He yanked his teeth from my arm, which flopped uselessly to my side as a warm, wet sensation settled over the wounds. I couldn't turn my head like Yutu had, but he climbed off me and scuttled away down the corridor.

Austin's face came into view moments later as he leaned over me, checking my pulse and turning my head. I managed a small grunt, which was the biggest relief I'd ever felt because it meant the venom wasn't long-acting.

When he lifted my injured hand, I nearly fainted. It was covered in blood and had multiple puncture wounds where the monster had skewered me with his teeth. If he hadn't been playing with his food, as he put it, I'd have already lost the arm, possibly more.

"You're alive," Austin said as he lifted me into his arms. My head drooped backward over his elbow. I desperately wanted to be able to stand on my own two feet, or at least tell him to go do what he could to save Ila.

I kept trying as he made it through the door to his room and lay me on the couch. He disappeared from view, and the sounds of furniture being dragged filled the silence. He reappeared shortly after with a hydropod and poured the water over my injuries before wrapping them carefully in bandages.

What I finally managed to say was, "*Should'veshothimtotheroof.*" By some miracle, he understood because he smiled.

"All I could think of was getting him away from you," he said, brushing back my hair.

"Venom freezes victim," I punched out carefully. My tongue felt like a nearly useless piece of rubber in my mouth.

Austin nodded. "It's wearing off. That's good."

"Ila—"

"I called for Nicole to come back for her. Jackson and Carter are outside already with Yang on shielded hovercots. We're barricaded in the room for now."

I relaxed back into the couch, sore from fighting so hard to move and communicate.

"I'm going to take advantage of this situation you know," Austin said with a smirk.

Hopefully, glaring daggers communicated what I thought of that.

"I mean I'm going to talk to you, and you have to listen," he corrected.

Fine. I gave him permission in my head, so I'd at least feel like I had a choice.

Austin lifted my legs, sat on the sofa, and dropped my feet in his lap.

"You were right," he said.

Good start, I thought.

"I keep trying to take charge, but nobody elected me." He looked up at the ceiling then back at me. "It's my defense mechanism, I guess. It's the way I know to protect myself, and it works really well. I know this because I'm still alive. But it sucks when it comes to trying to protect those I love."

He stopped and watched me as the word sunk in. I guessed it did exist, just like cryptids. But I'd be damned if I sought them out anymore. I felt the smile spread across my face, but I didn't try to interrupt.

"I wasn't listening to my own advice," he continued. "I'm supposed to live in the now, here in this moment, because it's all we really have. But when I had these feelings for you, they made me want to protect you and keep you with me forever."

His blush was adorable as he played with the fingers on my good hand. Sensation crept into my limbs as he spoke, letting me know the venom was wearing off. But I didn't move. I didn't want to interrupt him. "I stopped thinking about the now—the actual moment with you—and instead I thought of securing the future. So

I'm not going to do that anymore. I'm going to respect and trust you to make your own decisions because I love you, and because I know that's the only way to guarantee more possible nows with you."

Slowly, I propped myself up on my elbows and shimmied until I was completely in his lap. I wrapped my good arm around his neck, pressed my forehead to his, and kissed him.

It was slow and tentative at first as he let me take the lead. But the taste of him wiped away the feeling of Yutu on me. I pushed forward, sweeping my tongue across his to remind myself what a real kiss felt like. When I felt him poking me beneath my thighs, I pulled back.

Who knew about the future? He was right. But in this moment, right here? I loved Austin Cooper. And I told him so.

"I owe you an apology as well," I admitted. "Accepting your help doesn't make me weak. It makes me smart. I was just so used to fighting to be believed and dealing with thick-headed people that I guess it became an auto-response."

"I can be thick-headed." Austin pressed his forehead to mine to demonstrate, and I laughed.

"From now on we work as a team," I promised.

"We need to get him to the track. We only have an hour left," he said, bringing us back to the task at hand.

"He wants me. Bad," I said.

"But he's terrified of the guns."

"And the crystals." I wished I hadn't lost my bag when Yutu attacked.

"He's a coward. He likes to inflict fear in his victims, probably feeds off it, but he can't take what he dishes out."

I nodded. "He's a classic bully, but to the extreme."

"So I'll find him and lead him up to the top," Austin said.

My body slumped with disappointment. "Austin, I thought we'd been through this. He wants me."

"I know." He knocked his forehead against mine and stroked my face. "So you'll be his prize up there since you can't climb fast enough. But you have to get up there and hide the others. He can't have a sense that anything else is threatening him or he won't take the bait."

Austin pulled out what looked like a stun gun and handed it to me. "Here. Take it. You can defend yourself this way."

I started to protest.

"And protect the others," he added so I'd stop. "I'm going to use my acting skills. People hire me for to act all the time even though it's not what I love to do. I hear I'm pretty good at it."

I kissed him again, for luck, before standing. "Don't let it get to your head. But how are you planning to draw him out again?"

Austin deflated. "I don't know. I've been trying to think of something that would lure him out. But I've got nothing."

"I have an idea," I said, the excitement of a new plan bubbling up inside me. "He keeps talking in my head. What if it works both ways?"

32

AUSTIN

I DIDN'T LIKE THE PLAN. PUTTING THAT MONSTER BETWEEN MYSELF and Rosi, then chasing it *toward* her? It went against every fiber of my being. Part of me hoped it wouldn't work.

The rest of me knew I had to trust her, and other lives depended on this. Time was running out while that lazy ass face spirit drained our friends.

"Are you ready?" Rosi asked, twisting her hair around her finger as she paced the far end of the corridor.

"Are you?" I asked, practically twitching. I glanced up at the ventilation access in the hall, above and to my right. I looked back at Rosi when she didn't respond. She'd stopped pacing and squared her shoulders.

"Places then. Let's do this." She stepped onto the hover disks we'd salvaged and closed her eyes.

Gripping the laser gun, I ducked back to the corner of the hall and into the shadows. The idea was to scare the creature toward where we wanted it to go. My spear was strapped to my back just in case, but we knew the gun worked to at least scare it, so why not use it?

Rosi's lips moved as she spoke to the thing in her mind. The way she squeezed her fists told me she was putting everything into this. Lip reading wasn't my strong suit, but the "Come get me" before she opened her eyes was unmistakable.

We waited in silence, Rosi breathing hard in anticipation of fleeing upward. There was only one more level on the interior. From here we could make out the faint glow from the blue lights on the track. As the minutes ticked by, it felt less and less likely that our plan had worked.

Then came the scrambling sound and the grunting we'd heard in the caves. I stared at the access point, and I swallowed, clearing my mind in preparation for the deadliest game I'd ever played.

The grate erupted, flying across the hall and landing with a clatter on the ground. I held my position as first the claws, then the head of the massive beast appeared. Rosi gasped, and I doubted it was pretend. The creature focused on her with a grotesque smile before scuttling along the wall, ceiling, and ground in a display that seemed purposely creepy.

Using the hoverpad, Rosi rose into the air and started for the center of the resort. The monster hissed and made as if to lunge. But it halted, and I dropped back against the wall.

It lifted its head as though scenting the air. "I don't think you called me for a game of cat and mouse. You asked me to come out, and as much as I want to believe you desire the exquisite torture I provide, I doubt that was the intent."

"I guess you don't want me then," Rosi said, glancing my way.

Shit.

"The thing is," said the monster as it crawled up the wall and to the ceiling, a touch closer to my hiding place. "Twice, your people have fired a weapon at me."

It dropped to the floor and sprang toward me. I fired until it knocked the weapon from my hand. The next moment, I flew through the air and landed on my back, skidding across the fake ice of the ground. Then it was on top of me, pinning my legs. The stench of rot and sulfur made it difficult to breathe.

"And it had no effect. So I no longer fear your weapons," the *atshen* said, leaning toward me, pointed teeth dripping toxin onto my chest as I struggled to throw it off. I swung a fist toward the ugly face looming above me, and it caught my hand, squeezing until I saw stars.

"Your little friend already surprised me once. I won't fall for that again."

Attempting to find leverage, I kicked and bucked, but the monster secured my arms and legs to the floor with its own, its strength unbelievable. Helplessness crept in along with panic when I found I had nothing left to fight with. I felt like a flea trying to bite a rhinoceros.

I closed my eyes, not wanting to watch as it bit my face off, but instead of feeling its needle-sharp teeth, it was knocked off me. Scrambling to my feet, I found Rosi crouched in the hall, dagger held out before her.

The monster rose to its full height, higher than the doorframes in the corridor surrounding it. It howled, clutching its arm where a viscous black substance oozed from a gash. Then it sprung toward Rosi.

"No!" I yanked the spear from the strap on my back and hurtled it at the space between the beast and its prey. It wasn't the smartest move to lose my weapon, but I couldn't let it hurt her.

The action forced it to jerk backward, and Rosi flew at me, knocking us both off the railing and into the air. The magnetic tech of the hover disks struggled to keep up, slowing our descent. We clung together. But the disks wouldn't hold us both for long.

"You saved me," I said. "Again."

"Don't thank me yet. We're headed the wrong way."

"Rosi," I said, taking her beautiful face in my hands. "You've got this."

I stole a quick kiss from her sweet lips and jumped.

33

ROSI

My scream echoed through the entire resort as Austin dove into the tank in front of the waterfall. Time froze, as did my breathing, until his head finally shot through the surface. He gave me a thumbs up, and I turned my attention back to the creature, only to find it had disappeared again.

"No. No, no, no. You are not getting away again." Pure frustration had me spinning in air. "Where are you, you asshole?"

I spotted him, or rather the way he distorted the air around him in some form of camouflage around the rocks a deck below me. He'd paused, probably deciding which of us to go after. I had to think like him. It was me he wanted to taste. Me he wanted to torture like his old victims. So why was he resisting?

I stared at the knife in my hand. *Oh.* Austin had said he was a coward. I needed to act more helpless.

I dropped the knife and squealed like it was an accident as it tumbled to the ground below.

"Rosi!" Austin yelled from where he hung over the side of the glass.

Good. If he thought I was in trouble that would make it more believable. I spun in the air again, and gasped, as though I was afraid Yutu would pop out of nowhere and get me. It was entirely possible after all, except that now that I knew what to look for, I could track his movements as he climbed higher.

That odd blur moved along the rocks of the waterfall. He'd taken the bait.

Slowly, I rose on the hover disks, circling and moving away from the rock walls as though I was still panicking. Yutu climbed higher, scuttling around in a dance with me that he didn't know I was aware of.

The track was just a meter or so above my head now. And that was when the camouflage came off and Yutu leaped at me like the animal he was, jaws open wide.

My scream was real as I, too, jumped, grasping the edge of the anti-grav track and swinging one leg over the top when he collided with me. His added weight caused me to slip and grasp for purchase, trying desperately to hang on.

But Yutu couldn't fly either, and he swung us both up and onto the track, tossing me down on the ground where I scooted backward.

"Do I frighten you, little girl?" he asked as he stalked forward, toying with me again.

I nodded rapidly as I took inventory of the scene. Toklo and Cora hovered in the air, unconscious, arms spread out and hair flowing around them like they were suspended in water. A green glow emanated from them and wafted in tendrils toward what appeared to be a giant of a man—the same relative height as Yutu but far more substantial. He sat as if deep in meditation, arms and legs folded before him. His toned body was that of a man who worked out with weights daily, but his head was the same as the *tupilaq* that Ila's grandfather created. This was the spirit come to life to finally fulfill its destiny.

Took you long enough, I thought.

To my astonishment, it answered in my head. *You have been helpful in bringing me my quarry. The ancestors thank you.*

"Enough fun and games," Yutu said, redirecting my attention just as I backed into a wall. "I'm starving."

He was on me so fast I barely had time to throw up my hands. But he shoved me to the side like I weighed less than a feather and bit my shoulder, this time so much faster than before.

The pain was blinding, but the shock probably protected me from some of it as he tore a hunk of flesh and muscle out, tossing his head back in ecstasy. My blood sprayed both us and the floor as the venom took instant hold of me.

I couldn't speak. I couldn't move. I could only stare at a monster as he chewed and savored...*me.* Inside, I whimpered and cried as his long tongue again snaked out and licked the blood gushing from the wound. *What the fuck is taking the* tupilaq *so long?*

Yutu opened his mouth to take another bite, and I tried to brace myself, praying I'd pass out when the wind sprung to life around us, whipping debris so hard that it pelted Yutu like hail. He backed away from me into a crouch.

"Who disturbs my meal?" He howled into the ferocious gusts of what felt like a full-on hurricane.

I couldn't look away or move aside as bits of random objects sprayed my face and the gaping wound at my shoulder. Through the chaos strode the vision of the man I'd seen meditating.

"No!" Yutu shouted, backing up toward the broken railing. "I am immortal now!"

The wind surrounding the *tupilaq* quieted, and his body quivered then separated into five smaller figures, each one shaped like a young girl. They spoke and moved in unison as they arced outward in a half circle to surround Yutu.

"You are not immortal," they said. "You've destroyed your soul in exchange for a hiding a place. But justice never rests, and we have found you."

Sinking to his knees, Yutu cradled his head in his claws and released a terrible sound that shook the ground beneath me. "You are my conquests, my prizes."

"We are your demise," echoed the girls.

My head grew lighter as I struggled to focus. The figures grew hazy, muddled, and I didn't know if it was due to my blood loss or the magic involved. Behind them, I spied Austin, climbing over the railing, spear in hand again. He knelt to check the pulses of Toklo and Cora, who had collapsed to the ground.

I wanted to call to him even though I knew how stupid that was. I supposed it was a good thing the venom prevented that.

"I destroyed you all once. I will do it again," Yutu declared, swiping a claw out and catching one of the figures in the neck. He continued pulling until he tore her head off and tossed it to the side where it rolled toward me, empty eye sockets staring.

This wasn't a human. There was no blood, and real girls had eyes, I kept assuring myself as the other four molded back into the figure of the *tupilaq*. It launched itself at the monster, and the two began to tumble in a mass of claws, sharp teeth, and limbs.

Green light flowed from the *tupilaq*, who was now a good two feet shorter than Yutu. It surrounded the monster, and he writhed against it even as he snapped and clawed at the man. Austin crouched low to the ground and made his way around to me, hover disks tucked beneath his arms.

It was clear from the look on Austin's face as he stared at my shoulder and hurried to pull off his shirt and press it to the wound just how bad my injury was. I wanted to yell that it hurt but couldn't. He lay next to me and held pressure against my shoulder as he brushed back my hair.

"You did it, Rosi. You led him to the trap and saved Toklo and Cora."

I'd have glared if I could. *Yeah, and got gouged by the cannibal. Yay, me.*

"You sacrificed yourself to give them a chance," he said, cupping my face and turning it away from the creepy battle to a much nicer view of a much nicer storm—the one in his gray eyes.

He'd sacrificed himself too, and I appreciated it. But had either of us done enough? The way Austin's face kept fading in and out, I wasn't sure I'd be around for the outcome.

34

AUSTIN

OUR LIVES DEPENDED ON THE OUTCOME OF THE FIGHT HAPPENING behind me, but all I could see were Rosi's eyes rolling up inside her head, her skin so pale compared to her usual caramel complexion. So much blood coated her side and the surrounding floor that I didn't know how much could still be inside her.

She had to survive. If she didn't, then none of this mattered. Suddenly, I knew without a doubt that even the asteroid hike would feel flat and lifeless without the sparkle of her chocolate eyes and bubbly personality.

"Don't you dare leave me," I whispered in her ear as I felt for a pulse. "We're a team, Rosi. I can't do this without you."

Faint and fragile, the flutter beneath my fingertips was real. But I had to do something soon because my luck wouldn't hold out forever, and who knew how long it took for a supernatural wrestling match to finish? It could be too late if I waited.

I slid her belt off her waist and secured my shirt to her shoulder, pressing firmly against the worst of the wound. Then I stood, scooping her onto two of the disks I'd taken from Toklo and Cora. They were alive but unconscious so didn't need the disks as much as we did in the moment. I stepped onto them and held Rosi's good side so she wouldn't slip away from me.

When I turned us toward the edge of the track, I found the way blocked by the battle between evil and...lesser evil? I couldn't call it good when it had threatened us all and nearly drained the life force from two people.

The *atshen* gouged a chunk of flesh from the *tupilaq*'s arm, but where it should have looked like Rosi's injury, instead it filled with blinding green light that seemed to burn the monster when it touched that spot. I wondered briefly if knocking them over the edge was feasible, but I couldn't risk it with Rosi in tow.

"I need to get us by them, Rosi," I said, smoothing back her hair.

Her head rolled to the side, and she blinked. Then she made a soft sound like she was trying to say something. I bent down and leaned over her to listen. Whatever it was must have been important enough to waste her energy.

"Pocket," she rasped before her eyelids fluttered closed.

I wasted no time reaching into her pockets in search of whatever she meant to share with me but found nothing. I could have screamed then. I very nearly did. But then I set her gently down and reached into my own pockets to come back out with a fistful of black stones and a microchip—the one that had been in me. I'd nearly forgotten that Cora had given the obsidian to each of us, or that I'd grabbed the chip before discovering the doctor's remains. Could these items be enough to help? I glanced at Rosi and was certain it was the stones she was trying to tell me to use. She'd said it was what saved me out in the tundra. Her gaze locked on the stones in my palm, and she slowly opened her mouth as wide as possible.

"You're a genius. Hang in there, Rosi."

Drawing a deep breath, I faced the battle and took stock of the situation. Time seemed to slow as I zeroed in on my target. It was more than just hitting the *atshen* because the stones were so small. Rosi had understood I had to find a way to make sure the crystals had time to do some damage, if such a thing was possible. She told me exactly what had to be done. Now I needed to find a way to execute her instructions.

Ripping the tiny magnet from the chip, I stuck it in my ear, figuring it was the closest thing to my brain.

In many of the sports I'd participated in, I'd had to work on my timing. Act too soon and I'd waste my only shot. Act too late and it was over before it began. So I waited and watched, miniature weapons clutched in my fist.

I focused as hard as I could on my feelings for Rosi. The love that burned inside me, the pain of the potential loss if I couldn't save her somehow. The grief and guilt I felt about Sara. I let it all out, a sob bursting from my chest. The emergency lights brightened to the point I had to close my eyes, then seemed to explode all around me. When I opened my eyes again, the two struggling figures had stopped fighting to turn toward me. I'd gotten their attention. Now I needed Yuto to open up.

Glancing to my right, I spotted the spear I'd brought with me. *That could work.* I scooped it up and took aim, letting it sail through the air harmlessly past the mottled chest of the monster.

The *atshen* turned to grin at me.

"You missed," he hissed and opened his jaw to laugh.

"Nope," I said as I hurled the stones into his gaping mouth.

His chin snapped upward as he automatically swallowed. Then his eyes grew large. Fear shone in them as he stumbled backward. The *tupilac* lunged, stabbing him with a dagger made of green light.

A horrendous howl tore the space around us, and I fell to my knees, hands over my ears. The *tupilaq* nodded in my direction then wrapped his muscled arms around the monster and launched them both off the side.

Stumbling to my feet, I rushed to look over the edge in time to see the *atshen* spread-eagle on the rocks at the bottom, black oozing out in tiny rivers on the ground surrounding him.

But then his body began to vibrate and quiver, like he was doing some kind of strange dance on the ground. Smoke issued from beneath and around him as he appeared to deflate before my eyes.

I didn't have time for this. I ran back to Rosi and, after resecuring the magnet so there'd be no more accidents, used the hover disks to lower us to the ground. By the time we touched down, all that remained of the monster was a puddle of what looked like sizzling tar and some sickly gray skin and bones.

The smell was so bad I worried it might be toxic, so I rushed Rosi down the hall to the medcenter. I quickly set her on a hovercot and put her in stasis to keep her alive until we could find a new doctor.

Not long after, Nicole marched in, flanked by a small army of robots with glowing red chests and rollers on their feet. I looked up from where I sat on the floor, head buried between my knees.

"She needs medical attention," I croaked. "And you should check on Toklo and Cora, but last I saw them they were just unconscious. Their heart rates were steady, and I could find nothing obviously wrong with them. I had to help Rosi before she lost too much blood, and I didn't want to move them in case there were broken bones."

Nicole nodded and motioned to the robots to go to work. I rose, intending to follow along behind as they guided Rosi from the room. Thrusting out a hand, Nicole stopped me in my tracks.

"I want you to talk to someone after this, Austin," she said softly, so softly I did a double take.

As exhausted as I was, I found it impossible to ignore the vulnerability in her face. And it was the idea that she could be letting her impenetrable shields down for a moment that convinced me to let them take Rosi and hear her out.

"To who?" I asked.

"My therapist."

The laugh escaped before I could stop it. I wasn't sure if it was funnier that she wanted me to see one or that *she* did. To her credit, she waited until I quieted without reacting.

"When everything went down on Paradise Atlantis, I thought I was impenetrable. I handled it all quite well, dealing with each crisis as it arose and keeping those around me focused. But afterwards..." She looked away, and I believed she was seeing something from a year earlier. "The dreams came."

"I'm sorry," I said, placing a hand on her arm.

She looked back at me and smiled. "None of us are invincible. I suspect you think, like I did, that you are the professional here and that this was something you were prepared for. But take it from someone who knows. No one was prepared for this."

I nodded, swallowing back my objections. She was right, and maybe, just maybe a therapist could help me deal with having lost Sara as well. But first I had to make sure Rosi was going to make it through. Because if she didn't, there was nothing in the world that could help me handle that nightmare.

I started to leave but turned around at the last second. "This may not be the time, but may I offer you a business proposition, Nicole?"

35

ROSI

W<small>HEN</small> I <small>OPENED MY EYES</small>, A<small>USTIN WAS RIGHT THERE, HOLDING MY</small> hand. I startled him when I squeezed his fingers. He leaped to his feet then settled back down again to lean over me. The love in his eyes was almost too much for me.

"Who won?" I asked.

His smile told me all I needed to know, and relief swept through me. I tried to hug him and pulled back almost immediately.

"My arm works!" I held both out in front of me, marveling at them. "It doesn't hurt anymore."

"It took a few days, but they fixed you up. There's barely a scar thanks to the Bennets' doctors."

Frowning, I tugged at my hospital gown to peek at the crooked white line embedded in my shoulder.

"So sexy," Austin purred, and I couldn't believe the reaction between my legs.

"The effect you have on me is insane," I said with a sigh. "How long have I been out?"

Gently stroking my cheek, Austin informed me it had been nearly a week since I'd lost consciousness.

"Cora?" I asked.

"She's fine. So is Toklo. The only one with lasting injuries is Carter, but apparently, he's pretty excited about his new cyberlimbs."

"And the *tupilaq*?"

"I honestly don't know. He disappeared after killing the *atshen*."

I nodded, taking in the information. "I suppose he was no longer needed once his purpose was served. I won't mourn his loss, but I am grateful that he was there. Still, there were humans that did suffer. The doctor—"

"I know. I wish I could have gotten out of the machine sooner." Austin glanced at the wall, and I turned his face back to me.

"I'm relieved that you weren't hurt. If you had been, we couldn't have done it. The whole resort and everyone in it would have perished."

"It took both of us," Austin agreed. "We make a great team, Rosi."

I beamed back. I couldn't help it.

Then reality set in, sinking me back into my pillow.

"What is it?" Austin asked, coming to sit on my bed. "Should I call the doc?"

"No. It isn't physical," I said. "It's just... Vacation's over. I don't want to go back to California."

Straightening, Austin took my hand in his and turned it over to examine it as he spoke.

"Then don't go back. Stay with me. Like I said, we make a good team."

"Stay with you?" I repeated. It wasn't as though the idea didn't appeal. But— "I want to be with you, Austin, but I need to figure out what I want from life now that I don't have a driving need to prove myself by exposing the existence of cryptids."

"Actually, there's someone who wants to speak to us about that."

Austin stood and rushed out the door. My heart raced as I

waited. I didn't like being alone when I had no idea where I was or what was happening, especially after what we'd been through.

Just when I thought I might get up and rush out of the room as well, Austin returned with Nicole Bennet and another man. Sitting up straighter, I glanced from one to the other as they approached, Nicole's heels clicking on the tile floor. The tall, blonde man felt familiar.

"Glad to see you awake, Miss Sanchez," Nicole said. "I'd like to introduce my brother, Mason."

Of course. I'd seen his face on holos plenty of times, but he'd kept away from the limelight since the Paradise Atlantis incident.

"Nice to meet you," I said, trying to be polite while wearing no more than a paper hospital gown.

He had a brilliant smile. It felt more genuine than Nicole's and put me at ease.

"You sure you don't want to wait until you're up and dressed?" He looked from me to Austin to Nicole and back.

"We're good." Austin slid in next to me on the bed, throwing an arm around my shoulders and crossing his long legs at the ankles.

I had to laugh as I nudged him with my shoulder. "Okay then. I am curious."

"Mason is in charge of the environmental wing of Bennet Systems," Nicole said. "When I told him what you specialize in, and how you helped with our situation, he wanted to meet you."

"Actually," I said, face burning, "I won't be returning to my doctoral studies."

"That's helpful," Mason said.

I blinked.

"It'll be easier to convince you to work for us," he continued. "Knowing creatures and other beings exist in the small bits of wild we still have left necessitates trying to find, study, and help them as we encroach on their habitats. Or in the case of what happened here, avoid danger for ourselves."

"I don't see how—"

"Let him finish, please?" Austin whispered, and I fell quiet, crossing my arms.

"Finding and documenting these creatures will take research, prior knowledge, understanding, and empathy. It will often require physical challenges as well, which is where Austin comes in. Basically, I want the two of you to find, study, report, and field suggestions as to how to handle any cryptids you may find. We will then take the data and act on it in the most environmentally positive way. As you may know, I have considerable resources to put toward these efforts. So equipment, travel, lodging, and basically any needs are a nonissue."

Trying to digest this information made my head spin. He was offering me a job. Not just a job, but a new life with Austin doing what we both loved. We wouldn't have to worry about money or really answering to anyone but each other.

"I need some time to think," I said. "Not that I don't appreciate the offer."

Nicole clamped her mouth shut like she was afraid she might blow up if she left it open. But Mason smiled. "No problem. It's a lot to take in."

He steered his sister out of the room. Alone at last, I glanced at Austin as I twisted a chunk of hair. I almost put it in my mouth but thought better of it, realizing it hadn't been washed in far too long.

"You had something to do with this," I said.

"Maybe."

"Look, I want to be with you. But do I still love hunting cryptids?"

Austin waited, silent and filled with far too much patience as I worked on the information in my head.

What we'd just been through was horrific, terrifying, and dangerous. But I'd enjoyed every moment of it. I liked the adrenaline rush, working out problems in the moment, and all the amazing information I took in that no one had ever put together before. It excited me.

What did that say about me? That, I'd have to unpack later, but for now, I knew if I spent the rest of my life going from adventure to adventure with Austin and gathering real facts about these fascinating parts of our reality... Well, I was sold. And with Mason's backing, I'd have the resources, the equipment, and the support I needed to pursue actual documentation. Then whether others believed me or not didn't matter. It was enough that I knew and could present the truth to the world.

But that was all me. What about Austin? I narrowed my gaze, taking him in as I considered his situation.

"What about the asteroid hike?" I asked. "All of your daredevil adventures and extreme sports?"

Austin grinned. "That's the beauty of it. I can still do those things but with you, backed by Nicole. And the truth is, I never needed the publicity. That was just a way to fund my lifestyle. Doing this gives me the same thrill. Trust me, I proved that to myself these past couple of weeks."

I climbed up on my knees and kissed him. It felt like coming home, which was funny because I'd never really felt at home anywhere since I was a kid.

"Austin," I said, pulling back.

"Yes, babe?" he asked, stroking the small of my back.

"This? You and me? It's amazing, but it's all happened so fast. What if it doesn't last?"

He tilted his head and looked me in the eye. "When I do something, I do it all the way. And when I take a risk, I prepare ahead of time, but I trust the moment I start that it's right. And not to brag, but so far, my track record is perfect."

"I see. In this scenario I'm like...Everest. Or cliff diving."

Austin chuckled. "You are so much more. All of that? It was training for you, Rosi. I have a feeling you'll keep me in a constant state of wonder."

"No pressure."

"Maybe a little? Right here." Austin guided me to straddle him and pressed down on my hips as he bucked, hard and ready, against my core.

I gasped at the suddenness, but my body heated up immediately, the ache between my legs hungry for him. I was conveniently naked beneath my hospital gown.

"Do you feel up to it?" he asked in that husky voice that turned me on. "I can be gentle."

"What if someone walks in?" I answered, sliding against him.

"Weren't you the one who said the risk of discovery during sex was an extreme sport? I do like danger," he said, burying his face in my neck. His hands slid up my paper gown and his thumbs found my nipples, circling them slowly.

Fuck danger, I just needed him inside me.

Reaching down, I unzipped his jeans and released his impressive cock, cupping the shaft before guiding him inside of me.

"Oh God, Rosi, you're wet and ready."

He stated the obvious, but I still appreciated the way his eyes glazed over when he said it.

In answer, I rocked my hips, setting the pace hard and fast. I relished the sensation of him filling me so completely, hitting every nerve ending, sending electric currents of pleasure coursing through my body. More. I needed more of him. I couldn't get enough.

As if reading my mind, he flipped me over onto my side and lifted my leg to insert himself at an angle. Once again, the position was new and felt amazing as he thrust. I grasped at the stiff white sheets, pulling them from the bed like I could climb my way toward the orgasm building inside me.

Cries of ecstasy tore through my throat as I climaxed. Austin's deep grunt answered as he finished as well, collapsing against me and kissing my neck. "Those sounds you make take me over the edge, Rosi."

"You bring them out of me," I said as I caught my breath, sweat covering our bodies.

He thrust again, half hard and still inside me, making me squeal. Then he pulled out , brushing my hair from my face.

"I'm glad hospitals don't use IVs anymore," I said. "Can you imagine if we had to navigate with cables and tubes?"

Austin laughed. "We'd figure out a way to make that fun." He cupped my ass, hanging out of the open paper gown, and squeezed.

"Let me get dressed and we'll tell Mason we officially accept his offer," I said, rolling over to kiss him again.

"Or we could stay here and discuss a bit longer," he said, butting his forehead against mine. "I'm enjoying our lively debate." He ripped away what was left of my gown and squeezed my breast, immediately awakening the insatiable desire in my core again.

"I need a shower," I groused.

"Change of plans then," Austin said with a smirk. "We have a little more fun here, accept the offer, then get you to my place where we take our time getting every crevice nice and clean."

I bit my lip and whimpered before answering, "Deal."

Our discussion ended with his hand between my legs and me gripping the metal headboard above me as I came undone for him all over again. After we finally got dressed, spoke to Mason, and made our way to Austin's penthouse apartment, my head was spinning.

He lifted me into the air and twirled me around until I laughed. Then he set me down slowly, letting my body slide along his until my toes touched the ground, and our mouths connected yet again.

After a long, lazy kiss, I pulled back with a contented sigh. "I don't know how I'm going to get any work done with you around. Mason might as well pay us to fuck."

Austin laughed, and his body shook against mine. "I promise to control myself for eight hours a day." He lifted his hand in a scout's honor.

I smacked his chest. "That's all of a break I get?"

Pulling me tighter to him, he lowered his head and used his panty-dropping voice. "You can have whatever you want from me whenever you want it, Rosi. We're partners now in every way. If something is too much, just tell me and I'll stop. Always."

"What if I don't ever want you to stop?" I asked, already craving him between my legs again.

"Then I never will."

EPILOGUE
NICOLE

I knocked before entering Sam's quarters even though I'd wasted enough time setting up Austin, Rosi, and Mason for their meeting. Thankfully, my soon-to-be sister-in-law let me in almost immediately, her cerulean eyes shining almost as brightly as the giant diamond on her left hand, courtesy of Mason.

"I found her!" she exclaimed, dragging me inside by the wrist. She had three floating holopads set up above a clear keyboard she'd unrolled along the glass coffee table. She and Mason had a standing suite at the New York offices, same as all the family members. She deserved it not because of Mason, but because if it weren't for her, we all would have died below the ocean because of Bennet Systems' former VP.

"You found Candice?" I asked, sitting beside her to examine the holoscreens filled with maps and various blinking lines.

"It has to be her. She has the technical know-how, and theoretically the money after working for your mom for so many years in such a high position," Sam said, redoing her ponytail to keep her long blond hair from her face. "We know she's psycho, hates your family, and would do anything to ruin you, no matter how many lives she destroys doing it."

"But we've searched the entire planet and haven't found her," I said, trying to temper my own excitement at finally cornering the bitch responsible for killing so many and nearly shutting down all of Paradise Atlantis, the first Fantasy Resort.

"That was the problem," Sam said with a smirk, turning the screen on the far right to show me something. "She's not on the planet."

A yellow dot blinked at me from the center of a line of satellites not a thousand meters from where our next resort opening was slated to be. Candice was right next door to the Big Bang resort and no doubt already wreaking havoc. I clenched my fists so tightly the tips of my nails drew blood. So I grabbed a napkin from below Sam's half-drunk coffee cup and pressed it to my palm.

"You're amazing," I said. My praise was not given lightly, and Sam knew it. She beamed back at me.

"Should we call whoever's at the BBR to go get her?" she asked.

"No." I shook my head, glaring at the yellow dot and wishing I could set Candice on fire from afar. "It's too dangerous. We need to be smart about this. She can't know we're on to her or she'll run again. This time we use her own tricks on her. We will take her out when we prep for the space games. Only a select group of preapproved employees will be there, and they'll have the opportunity to back out if they feel it's too dangerous. We need to set her up."

"Won't it be obvious if we all show up to prep?" Sam asked. "You know we'll want to be there for this."

"I wouldn't dream of getting in your way of revenge, sweet sister. I plan on inviting all those she's endangered, from Paradise Atlantis to the Time Capsule Resort to our newly hired friends from Greenland."

"Who did you have in mind *exactly*?" Sam asked, sliding the holo back toward her before poising her hands over the keyboard. "I don't know how I feel about inviting Travis."

"Not who so much as what," I said, ignoring her mention of the psycho beefcake that nearly tempted her away from my brother.

The plan took shape slowly as I tapped the edge of the glass table. "How would you feel about getting married in space?"

Sam's mouth dropped open. "Oh, uh, Nicole, I don't think we want our wedding to be a trap for a serial killer. No offense. My kind of revenge is just watching her be taken away in handcuffs."

I grinned. "It doesn't have to be the real wedding. Just make her think she has a chance of crashing the happy occasion so your handcuff fantasies can become real. Not that Mason wouldn't try his best on that front."

Sam frowned at my insinuation as she thought it over. But I knew I had her. She wanted that bitch caught as much as I did. Maybe more. After all, she'd been drugged into helping her commit crimes and reprogram the AI. Surely, Sam would be willing to do almost anything to catch the crook.

"I think I can convince Mason," she said finally.

"Excellent. In that case, I'm happier than ever about the name we chose for this location."

"Why is that?" Sam asked with furrowed brows.

"Because Candice is going down with a big bang."

Thank you for reading! Did you enjoy? Please add your review because nothing helps an author more and encourages readers to take a chance on a book than a review.

And don't miss more from Lizzy Gayle with <u>THE BINDING STONE</u>, available now. Turn the page for a sneak peek!

You can also sign up for the City Owl Press newsletter to receive notice of all book releases!

SNEAK PEEK OF THE BINDING STONE

The magic is palpable. It tingles as it radiates up and down my arms. My eyes snap open the moment I feel it.

I let the power drift over and through me, soaking it up like a human does sunlight. My fingertips crackle with it. Voices become clear now, and sounds assault my ears like daggers after the blissful silence of nothingness. I prefer to sleep. When I do, there is no need to think. Or remember.

Whoever dares disturb my century-long slumber will suffer my wrath. That's a promise.

"Really? Only ten?" The voice of a young man attracts my attention.

He is close, but my senses remain dulled from my sleep inside the gemstone, so I choose to be cautious, staying invisible to human eyes. His voice, warm like honey, soothes the edges of my anger. But some qualities can be deceiving. I know from experience.

"Jer, remind me not to bring you along when I buy a used car," comes the voice of another young man. "Your haggling skills need some serious work."

I stand in the center of a modern marketplace. It is small but cluttered, centered in front of a brick house with several people milling about the lawn and walkways. Whatever time I'm in, the women wear far less clothing than I remember. Near the outskirts of the unkempt grass, I spy a girl who is closest in appearance to me. A small child tugs at her arm, but the woman is distracted. A smile pulls at the corners of my mouth, and I quickly change from the draped fabrics of my last master's time, mirroring her outfit. I nod in approval. I'm going to enjoy this century.

Now to locate and destroy the source of the threat. It is not difficult. I follow the same girl's blushing gaze toward the honeyed voice I'd heard before.

"I'll take it."

He stands a mere table's width from me, and it is clear he is indeed the One. His aura glows like none of the others. A rainbow of iridescent colors pulsates and bleeds around him like a force field. This is too easy.

A gasp draws my attention. It's the young mother, frozen in a state of horror. I've seen that look before, so I follow her stare to find the toddler examining a flower growing in a crack in the concrete. A machine of some sort zooms toward her, so big it will surely crush the child in seconds. Time slows as I raise my fingers and invisible hands lift the young one out of harm's way, setting her securely back near her mother. No one has seen, save the woman who will likely never again be so negligent.

Focusing on the rainbow aura, I raise my hands. All it will take is one blast, directed at the handsome man busy handing a piece of green paper to an elderly woman. He will cease to exist. But I feel it as I let go, and even before it bounces harmlessly off his aura, I know. So I scream. It is not as though anyone can hear it. Not yet.

"Never figured you'd go for the whole bling thing," says the one with glasses and a dull, human aura. "Try it on."

I watch helplessly as Jer slips the ring on his middle finger. The large opal in the center gleams a little too brightly, and I tug at the choker around my neck, running my thumb along the matching stone. I hope the ten-paper is worth more than it appears. Why must I care so much for the innocent after all these years? If I'd let that machine crush the child...

No. I am not, nor will I ever be, one of the human Magicians. It is what sets me apart, and the only thing that may make up for some of my past sins. The ones that were within my control.

"Great. Can we go now please?" It seems by his rush that the friend does not like it here. I cannot blame him. My nose wrinkles up as I scan the rest of the market—a few scattered tables covered in odd objects, dusty boxes stacked and interspersed between them. Most things I don't recognize, but it all looks like junk to me. So how did I end up here? Just one more indignity to add to the list.

I trail behind as the two boys move away and down the wide street. The homes surrounding the market are similar to each other, yet closer together than in my last master's time. It saddens me to find far fewer trees and greenery to balance all the brick and mortar surrounding us as we walk.

The chilled wind carries the ozone-tinted scent and humid feel of a body of water nearby, which pleases me. It is refreshing after my sleep. I let my bare arms stretch out behind me, allowing goose bumps to prickle along my skin. A few buildings away, the men amble up the uneven brick walk, scattering fall's last crisp leaves from the single maple tree in front, before bursting inside the four-story rectangle. I've seen worse. Although I'm certain this "Jer" will be upgrading soon. I continue following them up creaking metal steps and into a small room, containing a sagging, cushioned seat big enough for two, a square table and chairs, a well-worn bed, dresser, and a desk.

"Do you think it's real?" Jer's friend inspects the ring.

"I don't know, Gabe. There was something about it. Like I couldn't put it down."

Of course not. You sensed the power. My power.

I suppose I should reveal myself. If I do not, the stone will force me, and at least this way I can have a little fun with the friend.

I loosen the invisibility and freeze Jer's friend before he can touch the ring. I will teach him not to touch things that do not belong to him. I grin and let my eyes glow green with power so there can be no doubt as to my nature.

My new master's reaction is immensely satisfying. About to sit in the chair near the desk, he spies me and misses, falling to the floor with a *thud*. His face is pale, his eyes huge as his gaze darts between me and his friend. I would not be surprised if he fainted. Instead, he licks his lips and clears his throat.

"Hel...hello?"

Well, that's different.

***

Don't stop now. Keep reading with your copy of <u>THE BINDING STONE</u>.

A thousand years of servitude left Leela more than a little jaded. The betrayal of the man she loved was only the beginning of the nightmare.

After centuries of abuse by greedy masters, her hope for freedom for herself and her fellow Djinn from the magical stones that bind them has dimmed to a barely-there glimmer.

But it hasn't yet been extinguished.

When the young, handsome, and idealistic Jered inadvertently becomes her new master, Leela wonders if his tenderness and concern may be real. He doesn't even realize that he's a magician and wields magic of his own. Despite her years of suffering, her heart begins to open to him. And the chance of romance.

As she inches closer to trusting Jered, the original masters she assumed long dead resurface. They've found a way to survive, using young magicians' bodies to hold their essence. And when they discover her whereabouts, they come for her—and Jered. If the evil ones succeed, then she'll once again be in the service of the man who betrayed her, this time forever.

In the past, her choices led to unimaginable suffering. Now, when freedom or an eternity of torture both loom as real possibilities, can she dare risk everything for love?

Please sign up for the City Owl Press newsletter for chances to win special subscriber-only contests and giveaways as well as receiving information on upcoming releases and special excerpts.

All reviews are **welcome** and **appreciated**. Please consider leaving one on your favorite social media and book buying sites.

Escape Your World. Get Lost in Ours! City Owl Press at www.cityowlpress.com.

ACKNOWLEDGMENTS

As always, I must thank the entire team at City Owl and Mystic Owl Press. My editor, Heather, for her sharp eye and attention to detail, Tina and Yelena for their support and positivity, and, well, everyone!

Thank you to my beta readers, Leslie and Katharyn, you hit the nail on the proverbial head and helped me get mine on straight. Sarah, Shona, Theresa, and Julie, thank you for cheering me on and believing in me.

My dear, crazy, wonderful family deserves thanks as well for putting up with me and the way I zone out and ignore everything else so I can write. Even the bunnies and the bird have been patient with me.

Most of all, I want to thank YOU, dear reader, who sticks with me and joins me for the flights of fancy in my head. I hope I continue to provide you with a fun escape. Don't be afraid to let me know your thoughts, I love engaging with readers.

ABOUT THE AUTHOR

LIZZY GAYLE loves paranormal so much, she lives it. She is both an author and a psychic. Between mothering her three kids, attempting to understand her rocket scientist husband, and consistently attempting to declutter her home (that she is convinced is a secret portal to a clutter-creating dimension), she does her best to use her creative gifts and share them with you. Lizzy is a people person so if you contact her, it will make her very happy and she will likely answer while possibly including pictures of her bunnies and/or bird. She has also been known to write Young Adult under the name Lisa Gail Green.

www.lizzygayle.com

facebook.com/authorlizzygayle

instagram.com/authorlizzygayle

ABOUT THE PUBLISHER

City Owl Press is a cutting edge indie publishing company, bringing the world of romance and speculative fiction to discerning readers.

Escape Your World. Get Lost in Ours!

www.cityowlpress.com

facebook.com/YourCityOwlPress

twitter.com/cityowlpress

instagram.com/cityowlbooks

pinterest.com/cityowlpress